BEST YOU

BEST YOU

A NOVEL

KEITH YOCUM

ISBN 979-8-9855345-0-4
eISBN 979-8-9855345-1-1

Cover design and typesetting by Stewart A. Williams

For Denise, the gentle wave

Love is weak when there is more doubt than there is trust, but love is most strong when you learn to trust even with all the doubts. If a thing loves, it is infinite.

WILLIAM BLAKE

1

Many strange things in life cannot be explained.

It is that way now, and it has always been that way.

Phillip Preston, a 36-year-old assistant bank manager, was about to experience an event that he could not anticipate. It would change his life.

A kind, thoughtful, earnest, and modest man, Phillip was worried this blustery morning about a boat. He rowed his tiny dinghy to his motorboat that was moored in a small New England cove.

As was his nature, Phillip participated in a spirited internal dialogue with himself.

I can't believe I left the boat in this long. It's October and it's still in the water. I should have sold it a while ago. Now, look at it.

Phillip stopped rowing and turned to stare at the twenty-foot powerboat as it rocked sharply up and down in the rough, grayish water. Bits of foam whipped up by the re-cent nor'easter floated by like tufts of dirty cotton candy.

The wind heaved him back toward shore, so he started rowing again.

It was Martha's idea for the boat. 'Everyone has a boat, Phil,' she said. 'Everyone.' I can't afford to keep spending money on it. I don't even like boating. It was for Martha.

It was difficult to row against the wind. Although he was in a protected cove, the post-storm wind sent waves smacking against the bow of the dinghy. He could feel spray on the back of his orange rain slicker.

Damnit. I'm going to be late for work.

He leaned hard into his rowing, each thrust was met by a corresponding spray of water on his back and neck.

He grabbed the gunwale of the boat to catch his breath. The dinghy and powerboat rocked in contrapuntal syn-chrony, making Phillip dizzy. He pulled the oars into the dinghy and tied it off to one of the cleats on the motorboat.

Phillip was not a physically graceful man. Martha said he was "goofy." So, it was not surprising to see him stand uncertainly in the dinghy while he held it tight against the hull of the boat. He crawled awkwardly over the railing and tumbled onto the deck.

He sat there for a minute to get his breath. Next to him were the remains of his expensive anti-seagull device that had blown down. It was advertised to keep gulls off the top of his canvas canopy by spinning in the wind. But Phillip was doubtful of its efficacy. The rotating device appeared to invite, rather than frighten. Teams of gulls regularly took turns defecating on his boat's top.

He had grown to hate seagulls.

Phillip got to his feet and held on to the railing. He had rowed to his boat early this morning to check on the mooring line. He had been warned several times that his boat's mushroom anchor was too light for his boat in a violent storm and could drag. He was also warned that his mooring line could fray as it rubbed against the bow of the boat. There were many things to worry about when you owned a boat. Especially if you didn't like your boat.

Phillip walked unsteadily to the bow, gripping the railing as he went. He sat on a cushioned area in front of the windshield and looked closely at the mooring lines. One of the rope lines was indeed worn.

Phillip stood and kneeled forward next to the main cleat and peered down at the blue and white mooring ball straining to hold his boat.

If he had not looked down at the water that morning things would have turned out differently for Phillip. It is said that a person is only capable of bringing their singular worldview to an inexplicable event. Indeed, the scaffolding supporting a person's life provides the only guidance on how to behave.

To be honest, it *was* strange what happened to him next.

He looked down and gasped, whipping his head up reflexively.

My god! Oh my god!

Phillip forced his head down to look at the mooring ball again. He squinted as if that would help mediate the sight before him.

Inches below the gray, churning water was the naked body of a woman. She rested on her back, rocking gently in the waves. Her face was slightly above the surface and her eyes were closed. Her long hair was tangled around the mooring ball.

Oh my god.

He looked down once more at the body, then raced to the stern and crawled into his rocking dinghy. Phillip untied the line so that he could pull the craft to the front by using the railing.

When he reached the bow, the water was very rough as the wind and small waves jostled the dinghy. Phillip winced as he looked down at the body.

Oh my god.

The woman's face appeared waxen and unreal, and he wondered suddenly if it was a mannequin. He stared at her pale breasts as they moved up and down with the body, while her lower extremities descended out of sight below. He reached out and timorously poked the woman's forehead.

It was squishy and he yanked his hand back. Again, he scanned the cove as if there was an answer in the surrounding geography for why there would be a woman's body attached to his mooring ball.

Call the police. Yes, call the police. Tell them a dead naked woman is stuck to your boat. Don't touch her. They'll know what to do.

He reached into his back pants pocket and fumbled for his phone. He pulled the dinghy a few feet closer to his boat and held the railing with his left hand while he dialed 911 with his right hand. Phillip was able to key in his passcode before the spray, the rocking of two boats, and the angry water conspired to make him drop his phone into the cove.

It happened so quickly he didn't realize it was gone. He looked furiously around the inside of the dinghy for it as it rocked.

Oh my god.

3

Helplessness is not a unique feeling, and Phillip certainly experienced this haunting fear before. But where some might lash out in anger or shrink into depression at such times, Phillip was of the other school. He sought self-control and self-reliance when stressed.

Phillip preferred order and regimen to seek relief from the many dissonant interactions he faced. Granted, his mild manner and accepting nature confused those around him. Some saw self-absorption and judgment in his behavior. In his youth, he was bullied. Bullying begets bullying, and Phillip was a consistent locus of that activity in his school years. In adulthood, his self-reliant nature and embrace of orderliness was gently mocked.

He accepted this opprobrium with well-honed restraint.

Yet, this windy and confusing morning tested Phillip's resolve.

Do something! Get her out of the water!

Phillip tied off the dinghy's line to a cleat and sat down in the small rocking craft. He looked at his watch. Phillip had ninety minutes to get back home, change his clothes and open the bank. As assistant manager of the bank, he had never failed to open it on time. It was his duty, and he was proud of his conscientiousness.

Phillip forced himself to look at the woman's face that rested at the surface, bobbing slightly. He used the mooring-ball line as a guy wire to pull the dinghy back to the body. The woman's hair was knotted around the top of the mooring ball where the boat line connected.

Phillip pulled and tugged at her hair, ripping it apart to free her. It was not pleasant to touch her body, but he forced himself to reach under her armpits and drag her beside the dinghy as it drifted back to the stern.

Don't look at her. Don't.

Indeed, it was disturbing, and he grimaced throughout the ordeal, avoiding even a casual glance at her. She was not easy to manage; her arms flopped to her side and he still could not see her legs since they were beneath her in the soupy, gray water. He was intent on not dropping her.

Rivulets of sweat rolled down his temples as he struggled with the bouncing dinghy and the heaving body. He managed to wrestle her onto the deck of the motorboat, keeping his eyes away from her body and focusing on other objects. Phillip lay flat on his back staring up at the gloomy sky. He felt dizzy and damp, so he sat up.

But he could not resist a small sideways glance at the body.

He gasped. His hands shot to his face, where he managed to put one of his fists into his open mouth.

Three feet away from him on the deck of his small powerboat lay the naked body of a woman resting on her side facing him. Her dark matted hair covered most of her face, and her white breasts moved slightly as the boat rocked. Salt water ran off her pale, muscular stomach.

It was the rest of her body that disturbed Phillip.

4

The body had no legs.

Below the waist was a single tapered body part covered in large green iridescent scales the size of silver dollars. The body part ended in a large flat fin.

Phillip scooted away from the body crablike until he was up against the small cabin door. Again, he scoured the surrounding cove desperately seeking an answer for the question that lay in the bottom of his boat. A joke, perhaps. A bad joke, perhaps. A sign of dementia. Early-onset dementia. Very early.

Am I having a nervous breakdown? The divorce? Of course.

Phillip calmed himself, breathing slowly and staring at his car parked on the shore nearby. He glanced at the body again, letting his eyes inch their way toward the woman's face. Her body moved slightly with the rocking of the boat.

The absurdity of her body was too much for Phillip and he opened the door to his small, cluttered boat cabin. He stooped in and fumbled past two fishing poles, four folding chairs in their bags, and a small grill. There was a folded blue tarp that he had in a storage compartment. He opened the cabinet and pulled it out.

He realized how tired he was, and he sat on the edge of the compartment.

I don't understand. I don't understand.

The boat rocked and he rocked with it, side to side, sitting inside the cabin. He stayed that way for several minutes. He was not eager to go outside to cover the body. He stared idly through the small starboard porthole at the gray light streaming through.

He looked at his watch.

I have to open the bank!

He stood, making sure to stoop as he made his way to the cabin entrance. He stepped out and up one step.

It was one step too far for Phillip. A strange day was to get stranger.

5

A live naked woman sat at the starboard corner of the boat, her back against the transom. She held her legs up so that her knees were at her chin.

"I'm cold," she said. "Very cold."

Phillip jerked back into the cabin, but not before his head clipped the top of the cabin entryway and rendered him briefly unconscious.

He thought he was swimming in a black ocean and preferred to stay there as long as he could

"You. Wake up."

Phillip opened his eyes into the face of the woman. She stood over him in the entranceway. He closed his eyes.

He felt a finger poke him in the chest.

"You!"

Phillip squinted. The woman leaned over, her face not more than twelve inches from his.

"Are you sick? Why do you sleep?"

He sat up on his elbows.

Many things were dancing around in Phillip's head, but he could only manage a couple of words, none of which made sense or were appropriate for the moment.

"What are you doing here?" he said.

"You left me out of the water too long," she said, looking around the cabin.

Phillip was not planning to see a naked woman that morning at his boat. She leaned over him, her pubic hair glistened with water droplets and her breasts swung back and forth with the rocking of the boat.

"Get away from me," he said.

"Get away? Look what you did to *me*!"

She slapped her two wet thighs with her hands.

"Look!"

He looked at her thighs, then up at her face.

"I don't know what happened. I hit my head. Why are you here?"

"Why? Because you left me out too long." She slapped her thighs again. He did not look at her thighs this time but kept his eyes on her face.

"Leave me alone," he said. "Go away. I have to open a bank."

She poked him hard in the chest with her finger. "I'm cold."

She stepped back and Phillip rolled slowly up off his elbows and sat forward. He stared at her bare feet.

"What happened to your other part?" he said. "You didn't have feet before."

"I tell you. You left me out for too long. Your fault."

"I don't feel well," he said, still looking at her feet. He swallowed hard.

"What is your name?" she demanded.

"Phillip."

"Alright Mr. *Fillleeeep*, get up. Can you not see I'm cold. Look at my skin. I got the bumps."

He saw that her arms and chest were indeed riddled with goosebumps. Phillip undid the zipper on his rain jacket and pulled it off.

"Here. Put this on."

She took it and felt the vinyl material crinkle in her hands.

"Give that," she said pointing at the sweatshirt he was wearing.

He tugged it over his head and held it out to her. She put it on, then put the rain jacket over that.

"Better," she said.

Phillip noticed that both the rain jacket and the sweatshirt fell to her waist but exposed the rest of her body. She did not seem to care and ordered him again to get up.

He stumbled out of the cabin, rubbing the back of his head.

This doesn't seem right. Something's wrong.

They stared at each other, both rocking with the boat.

"What are you goin' to do with me, Mr. *Fillleeeep*?" the woman said. She pronounced Phillip in a strange manner.

"I'll take you to the hospital. I don't have a phone. It fell in the water." He rubbed the back of his head. "I'm going to be late for work," he said, mostly to himself.

"I go with you Mr. *Fillleeeep*," she said, putting her hands on her hips.

"You need to go to a hospital."

"I go with you," she said.

"I'm sorry. I'm confused," he said rubbing the back of his head again. "But I really need to get you medical care."

"We go to home," she said.

"We need to go to a hospital. Something strange happened to you. They'll help."

The woman scanned the land around the cove, then

looked at the raised outboard motor. She rubbed her hands against its cowling.

"We need to get to land. Back to my car. Over there." He pointed to his car parked on the side of the road next to the beach.

"What is that?" she said.

"It's a car."

"You're the boss, Mr. *Fillleeeep*."

"Phillip is my first name. You can call me Phillip, not Mr. Phillip."

"You're the boss, *Fillleeeep*."

He managed to get the woman into the front of the dinghy while he sat on the small bench seat facing backward and started to row to shore. The wind was behind them and they reached the beach quickly.

The woman got out of the boat and stood in the water up to her ankles while Phillip dragged the dinghy up the beach, removed the oars, and turned the dinghy over on its back. The woman remained with her feet in the water.

"Are you coming?" he yelled above the roar of the wind and the lapping waves.

She seemed reluctant to leave the water.

"You are the boss," she said finally, walking up the beach.

He only wore a tee-shirt, sweat pants, and tall rubber boots. He worried about opening the bank building on time.

When they got to his car, she stared at it and rubbed her open palm against the driver's side door and window.

"You need to get in," he said, opening the door and sitting inside.

She stood next to him so that he could not close the door.

"Please, get in," he said.

She stooped and looked at the passenger seat across from him, then jumped in and crawled across him. Her bare knees dug sharply into his thighs and he yelled.

"Hey! Ouch. What the heck are you doing?"

She scooted onto the passenger seat, leaving a trail of sand from her feet sprinkled over his thighs and the car's center console.

I have to open the bank.

He started the car and she jumped.

"I don't like. Make it stop," she said.

"Can you put on your seatbelt please?" he said, strapping himself in.

"Make noise stop, *Filllleeeep.*"

"Hang on. We have to get going." He put the car in drive and accelerated onto the empty road.

She screamed. "Stop!"

"I can't stop," he said. "Close your eyes if you don't like it. I really have to get going."

She pulled her knees up to her chest and covered her eyes with her hands.

Her shrieking was only marginally louder than the pulsing alarm from the dashboard warning that her seatbelt was not attached.

Phillip looked at his watch.

I'm going to be late! I've never been late. Maria will tell everyone I was late. Mr. Sampson will find out. Why is this happening to me!

He took a glance at the woman. She had folded herself into a ball on the seat.

"No!" she yelled periodically.

"I can't stop," he said. "I really can't. It will be alright. You'll see."

He looked at his watch, made a quick mental calculation, and decided he had no choice.

7

He pulled into his driveway and hit the garage door opener. The woman moaned in agony the entire trip.

Phillip looked to see if any of his neighbors were outside and saw no one.

The car slid into the garage and he lowered the door behind him.

"We need to get out," he said, opening his door. She didn't move.

He raced around to her side and opened her door. She looked up and glowered at him fiercely.

"You are mean!"

"Please get out. Come quickly."

She stood up in the garage and looked around at the hanging garden tools, two bicycles, and assorted domestic items.

"Live *here?*"

"Well, not in the garage," he said, opening the door into the kitchen.

She followed him in as he raced down the hallway to his bedroom.

"Sit down and relax," he yelled.

He changed into his work attire of khaki slacks, a blue, button-down, long-sleeve shirt, and light-blue tie. He slipped into his brown loafers and raced down the hall to the kitchen.

Phillip entertained the briefest fantasy that the woman had disappeared.

People suffer breakdowns all the time. It was the divorce.

He was thrilled to find that, in fact, the half-naked woman *had* disappeared.

Oh my god. I feel so much better.

He grabbed the keys off the kitchen table and opened the door leading to the garage.

Leaning against the warm car was the half-naked woman.

"What are you doing here?" he yelled.

"I don't like," she said.

He looked at her pressed against the front of the warm hood of the car. She was still naked from the waist down.

"Please go inside," he said. "Sit down. Watch TV."

"I don't like," she said.

"I'll be home in a while. Go inside. You're freezing."

He opened the car door, jumped in, pushed the garage door switch and it groaned to life.

Phillip watched her race inside the kitchen door and slam it shut. He sat in the car while he looked at the kitchen door. He rubbed the knot on the back of his head. It was sore.

He started the car, backed out, shut the garage door, and raced to work.

8

Maria was standing outside the bank door when he pulled up. He waved and she waved back. Phillip was four minutes late.

He chose to walk to the front door at his normal pace; running would only accentuate the fact that he was tardy. Phillip was *never* tardy.

"Good morning Maria," he said.

"What a blow yesterday," she said. "We lost power. Did you?"

"No," he said, unlocking the front door. "I was lucky."

Phillip quickly stepped inside the empty bank, turned on the lights and raced to the alarm panel, and punched in the code.

He turned to watch Maria walk behind the counter and stash her purse and rain jacket in the small alcove.

So far so good. She didn't mention being late.

Phillip unlocked the large safe and took out the full cash tray for Maria and took it to her.

"Here you are," he said smiling.

"Thank you, Phillip," she smiled back.

He returned to his small office and sat down to gather his thoughts. He swallowed hard and bit the inside of his lower lip. He held out his right hand. It was steady at first, then it shook a little and he quickly lowered it onto the desk.

OK. Let's start the day over. You're at work. Maria is outside attending to the first customer who's at the drive thru. Things are normal. The Powells are due at ten o'clock to complete their home equity loan.

And the day was indeed normal for a Saturday. Maria was her normal chatty self, the bank customers came and went like they typically do, and Phillip was thrilled to lock the building up again at one o'clock in the afternoon, their normal closing time on Saturday.

"Enjoy the rest of the weekend, Maria," he said.

"You too, Phillip. Maybe the sun will come out."

"Ha, we can always hope," he smiled.

When he got into the car, Phillip suddenly felt dizzy. He thought of the naked woman in the water. He felt his palms grow moist as he mulled the events on his boat. He looked at the passenger seat.

I don't see any sand. There was no woman in that seat.

But there was a little sand on the seat. He bent over to look at it. He brushed it off.

That's old sand. Don't get carried away.

He started the car and drove to the mobile phone store

to get a new one. He had purchased insurance on his phone at Martha's insistence.

"Phil, everyone loses a phone or drops it on the floor," Martha had teased him. "Don't pinch every penny you have!"

Perhaps he was a penny pincher and needed to loosen up a bit. He bought insurance on the phone that was now nestled in the eel grass at the bottom of the cove.

The transaction and backup of data on his new phone went smoothly at the store. Phillip then stopped by the little diner at the corner of Main Street and Hawthorne Avenue, where he typically had lunch on Saturdays after closing.

He sat on the little red swivel stool at the counter.

"Big storm yesterday," Muriel said as she poured a cup of coffee for him. "You still got your boat in the water? Most boats are out this time of year."

Phillip felt a tingle of electricity run up his spine at the mention of his boat.

"Yes. I'm afraid I've been a tad lazy this year," he said taking a sip. "I should have pulled it. I'm calling the marina today."

"Well, don't delay. I heard there's another blow coming next week."

"Oh, jeez. I'll call today. Thanks."

"You want the regular?" Muriel said.

"Yes please."

Four stools down on Phillip's right sat Henry Holt, the 84-year-old former town selectman.

"Hey Henry," Phillip said.

"Hey there young man," Henry responded.

Phillip stared at his black coffee and could see his reflection on the smooth surface. He felt tired. He took another sip.

"You hear about the library?" Henry said, his voice wavering slightly with age.

"No, Henry I didn't."

"That big oak out front blew down on the library last night. A lot of damage. Got the whole DPW out cleaning up the mess. That oak must have been two hundred years old."

"That's too bad. It was a fine tree," Phillip said.

"It was a black oak."

"I see," Phillip said.

"Kinda rare out this way. We got mostly the white oak."

"I didn't realize that."

"Kinda rare."

Muriel brought Phillip his grilled cheese sandwich on a thick, well-used white porcelain plate.

"You gonna have chips today?" she asked.

"I don't think chips are good for you," he said.

"You always say that," Muriel said.

"I suppose I do."

"And then you eat them when I put them next to you," she said.

"Yes, I suppose that's correct."

"If I didn't put them next to you, you wouldn't eat them."

"That's probably true."

Muriel, at five feet tall, was a rotund fifty-year-old widow that took over the diner when her husband died of a heart attack four years ago.

Phillip liked Muriel because she never asked him about the divorce. She kept the conversations simple. He appreciated her habit of just standing on the other side of the counter and not saying a thing.

She pushed a small bag of potato chips toward him in painfully slow motion, an inch at a time until the bag was three inches from his plate.

Phillip stared at the bag.

"They're bad for you," Phillip said.

She nudged the bag one inch closer to his plate.

"Lord," he said, grabbing the bag. "I don't know why I let you do that."

"Because you like 'em, that's why."

He tore the bag open and popped several into his mouth. Muriel went down the counter and commenced chatting with Henry.

Phillip took longer than normal to finish his lunch.

There's no one there. How in god's name can that woman be there? You were having a breakdown. But look. You opened the bank on time. Mostly on time. You're at lunch. You got a new phone. Things are normal. Go home. Take a shower and get that salt water smell off you.

9

Phillip pulled the car into the driveway and stopped before opening the garage door.

Stephen Cornish, his retired neighbor, was in his front yard across the street raking up the storm debris when Phillip drove by. They waved at each other.

Phillip stared at the garage door as the car purred. He reached up to the visor and pushed the door opener. The door rose and the panels folded up into the rack. He drove slowly in and parked, lowering the door behind him. He turned off the engine and waited.

Phillip did not like the feeling of fear and confusion. He stared at the kitchen door but did not get out of the car. His palms were moist again and he wiped them on his thighs. He felt his phone buzz and he pulled it out of his rear pants pocket.

It was a text from his sister.

lost power last night. u?
no. was lucky. Just got home from work
u coming to dinner tonight?
i don't know
can't wimp out phil. u promised
tired. will check in later
i will come and get u
talk later
grrrrr

He got out of the car and walked to the kitchen door. He placed his hand on the doorknob but didn't turn it. After several seconds he removed his hand and stood back. He swallowed, cleared his throat, put his hand on the door, and opened it.

He did not enter directly but poked his head in and looked around. The house was silent, except for the battery-powered wall clock next to the refrigerator. Phillip hated that clock. It made an audible tick as the second hand stuttered around the dial. He would offer it to Martha perhaps. Or drop it at the dump's leave-and-take section.

He stepped in and closed the door gently behind him. The house was exactly how he left it, minus the half-naked woman. He walked into the family room to the left, then walked down the hallway to the two bedrooms. He looked into the spare bedroom. Nothing.

He crossed the hallway and looked in his room. Nothing.

He sighed. His shoulders sagged as relief swept over him. Phillip sat on the edge of his bed and removed his shoes, socks, shirt, tie, and finally his khakis. He rubbed his eyes as if he were removing a film of dust. He sat in his boxer shorts and debated whether to take a nap.

He walked out of the bedroom and into the bathroom at the end of the hallway.

10

"Hey!" he yelled.

She was lying naked in the empty bathtub fussing with the downspout.

"*Fillleeeep*, the water," she said pointing at the faucet. "Where?"

He backed up slowly and re-entered his bedroom. He sat down on his bed and flopped back, closing his eyes.

There was a thump as her feet hit the floor. She came down the hall and entered his room.

Phillip kept his eyes shut.

I don't feel well. I don't like any of this.

"You sick?"

He didn't answer and kept his eyes closed.

The bed sagged as she sat down.

"You." She poked him in the ribs.

He ignored her.

She poked him much harder.

"Ow. Stop it," he said. "Go away."

"Cold," she said.

"Stop talking to me!" he said sitting up. There was much tumult swirling through Phillip's brain. "I can't talk to a strange, naked woman on my bed," he said out loud to himself.

"Cold, *Fillleeeep.*"

"You're cold because you sat in an empty bathtub. Why don't you just leave me alone."

"Are you a good boss or bad boss?" she said, shivering.

"I'm not your boss."

"You left me out too long. *Fillleeeep* you now the boss. It is always that way."

"What are you talking about! For god's sake, would you please get dressed? Put something on." He flopped back in bed and stared at the ceiling.

Now, it must be said that Phillip was modest in his personal moral code, to the point of prudishness. The woman's naked body troubled him, and her unselfconscious behavior was difficult to reconcile. Should *he* not be the angry one demanding answers? Instead, *she* was the aggressor. How could that be?

"You don't like women."

"Who said I don't like women?"

"Why you not look at me, *Fillleeeep*?"

"It's not normal to walk around naked."

"You are baby," she teased.

He bolted out of the bed and walked down the hallway to the kitchen. He felt foolish in his boxer shorts, but the entire day was foolish. He opened the refrigerator and took out a Diet Coke and opened it.

The woman puttered down the hallway and entered the kitchen.

"I'm cold," she said.

"I'm not going to talk to you."

"Talk to me."

"No, I'm not."

"You baby."

"Stop calling me a baby."

"I'm cold."

"Well," he said turning to her, "you're naked. What do you expect?"

"Don't like cold."

Phillip turned away, took a big gulp of Diet Coke, and opened the refrigerator.

"Hungry *Fillleeeep*. You have eating things?" She rubbed her wet stomach in a circle with her open hand. "Many hungers inside."

She twisted her mouth into a sort of woe-is-me look.

Compounding Phillip's problem was the woman herself. She was beautiful in a striking, unconventional way. She was just over five feet tall, had light-brown hair that he had not yet seen dry. She had medium-sized breasts, a thin waist, and muscular thighs. Her pubic hair was dark.

But it was her eyes that were unusual. They were shaded a pale green with a strange piercing quality. Phillip had trouble looking at her face straight on because of the eyes.

"The hunger is inside *Fillleeeep*."

11

She stood next to him and they both stared into the open refrigerator.

"Is this your food thing?" she asked.

"Yes."

"It is cold inside," she said. "How?"

"It just is," he said. "It's too complicated to explain."

"Many hungers," she said.

"What do you want to eat?"

I don't believe I'm having this conversation.

"Green things?" she said. "You have green?"

Phillip reached down and pulled out the produce drawer. Inside were several heads of romaine lettuce in a plastic bag.

She picked one up and held it to her nose, sniffed it loudly, then took a timorous bite. She chewed it slowly.

"You like?" she said.

"Let me wash it for you," Phillip said taking it out of her hand and walking to the sink. He rinsed it off and then dried it with a paper towel.

"I'll let you have this," he said holding it in his hand up in the air, "if you get dressed. You shouldn't walk around naked."

"Cold," she said.

He handed her the romaine and said, "Follow me."

They walked down the hallway into the spare bedroom. Phillip opened the closet doors.

"She left these behind," he said pointing to clothes on hangers.

The woman stared at the clothes, chewing on a leaf of lettuce.

"You've never worn clothes before?" he said.

She did not answer and looked confused.

He shook his head.

"I don't feel well," he said.

"You sick?" she said.

Phillip grabbed a blue long-sleeve shirt, a pair of blue slacks, and a fleece vest from hangers. He threw them onto the bed.

"You can put those on," he said. "They were Martha's."

Phillip took the lettuce out of her hands and put it on the bed.

He held out the shirt and asked her to put her hands into the sleeves, then helped her with the buttons.

"Mmm. No bra. Oh well," he said.

"What?'

"Nothing. Now sit down on the bed and we'll put the

pants on. Crap. No underwear." Phillip went over to the dresser and looked in the drawers. They were empty.

"Most people wear underwear," he muttered. "Stay here."

He walked across the hallway to his room, opened his dresser, and pulled out an unopened package of white jockey underwear. He ripped the package and returned to the spare bedroom.

"Here. Put these on first. I'll show you."

She sat down and he got to his knees in front of her and put her feet into the open holes. He asked her to stand and directed her to pull the jockey shorts up.

She grimaced. "Feel funny," she said. "Do I have to wear, *Fillleeeep?*"

"Yes."

She reached down and played with the front pocket of the men's underwear, poking her fingers through from the inside.

"Don't ask," he said. "Now, sit down and put your legs through each of the pant legs. Then stand up and you can button them at the top."

She did as she was told but managed to devour a lettuce leaf quickly.

"You look fine." He walked back to the kitchen and sat down.

12

Phillip's confusion about the day's events drained him of energy. Behind his confusion was a hint of fear—was he falling apart?

People under immense stress sometimes fall apart. But Phillip had never fallen apart, though he had his share of life's stresses. He relied on his unique psychic scaffolding to prevent meltdowns: he was nonconfrontational by nature, avoided interpersonal conflict, and accepted uncomfortable events with quiet acceptance.

He sat at his kitchen table in his boxer shorts drinking a Diet Coke. Sitting across from him was a strange woman that he had pulled from the water that morning. She was wearing some left-behind clothes of his former wife's.

He was either insane or not insane.

He chose not insane. This stressful event would pass, like the others.

She reached across the small table and grabbed the glass salt shaker.

"Can I have?" she said.

"It's salt."

She yelped with glee and grabbed the shaker. She shook it onto the lettuce head so that the crystals fell everywhere, covering the table top. She devoured the rest of the lettuce.

Phillip drank his Diet Coke in silence, staring down at the white crystals. He pushed a few of them around with the tip of his forefinger.

"What's your name?" he said.

"I don't know. I have lots."

"Just one will do."

"Let it be Sofia," she smiled. "I like. You like?"

"I guess. Do you have a last name?"

"No."

Phillip was calm now. His agitation and confusion had slipped away.

"*Fillleeeep*, why you sad?"

"I am?"

"Like a little puppy dog. You know puppy dog?"

"Yes."

"You like that. But bigger. And no tail."

Phillip barely heard her, consumed with the parameters of his new existence.

"Where did you come from again?" he said.

"Sofia. I like."

"No, I mean *where* did you come from, Sofia?"

13

"I don't know," she shrugged.

"You came from somewhere."

"I suppose."

"What were you doing in the water stuck to my mooring?"

"It was the storm. I get tired."

"Have you been stuck before from a storm?"

"Oh yes. Many storms."

Don't ask any more questions. You're going in too deep. Stay at the surface and you'll be fine.

"*Fillleeeep* been a long time since out of the water. I don't know things."

He guzzled the rest of his Diet Coke.

"What is that thing for?" she said pointing at the light switch on the wall.

He stood up and flicked it so that the light bulb blinked

over the kitchen table. He sat down.

"Ah. I like," she said.

"Just for the record," he said, "I don't believe anything that's happened so far."

"Can I have more green things?" she said.

"Of course," he replied. "But wash them before you eat them, OK?"

"Yes," she said jumping up and opening the refrigerator. She pulled out another head of lettuce and took it to the sink. Phillip watched her closely.

"Not that one," he said when she fiddled with one of the faucets to get water running. "That's for hot water. Turn the other one."

She followed his directions and returned to the table.

He looked at the clock on the wall while she poured out more salt so that the oak table top was covered with loose salt.

Phillip looked at her as she stuffed the lettuce leaves into her mouth.

"What happens to you now? How does this work?" he said, avoiding her green eyes.

She shrugged. "You're the boss. I work."

"And this has happened before?"

"Always after storm," she said, frowning. "Get tired."

"And someone finds you and keeps you out of the water?"

"Yes."

"And you grow legs?"

"Yes," she took another huge bite of lettuce.

"And then what?"

"Work. Always same."

"How many times has this happened to you Sofia?"

"Don't know."

"Ten times? Two times? A hundred times?"

"*Fillleeeep*, don't know!"

"When was the last time this happened?"

"Don't know."

"Who found you the last time this happened? A man or a woman?"

"Man. Big man."

"What did he ask you to do?"

"To clean boat, fix nets, things. And find firewood. Always firewood."

"Did he have a car?"

"Like your machine?"

"Yes."

"No machine."

"Did his boat have a motor or sails?"

"Motor?"

"Did it make loud noise?"

"No. Just the big white thing of cloth. No loud noise."

"He was a fisherman?"

"Suppose, yes."

"What else did he have you do?"

"Cook food. Wash things. Do the 'in-out' thing. Like that." She shrugged.

"The 'in-out' thing? What's that?"

"Oh, *Fillleeeep*. Men want to do the 'in-out' thing." She made a circle with her thumb and forefinger of her left hand and poked the forefinger of her right hand into the circle. "You know."

"That's disgusting," he said.

"All men want. Women who find me only want me work. Work, work, work. Men who find me want me to work, work and then the 'in-out' thing."

"That's disgusting."

She shrugged.

14

"So how do I return you?" he said. "Do I just take you back to the water?"

"Don't want me to work?"

"No, I don't need you to work."

"Can I clean your fish?"

"No, I don't need you to do that."

"I clean things. Get wood. You need firewood?"

"No. Can't I just drop you off at a bus station with some money? Or take you to a shelter?"

"Don't know what you mean."

He ran his fingers through his hair.

Why not just take her to a hospital? Or a shelter?

"*Fillleeeep,* you like me? I work, work, work." She smiled. "You are the boss."

So, Phillip, immersed in a strange world that left him untethered and unsettled, fell back on his only method for dealing with dissonance. It had never failed him.

He stared at her for a long time, and finally said, "So, we need a story."

"I like stories," she said clapping her hands in excitement. "Tell story."

"OK. It's like this Sofia. Someone I know said they knew a person looking for a short-term rental. And since I had a house, I decided to rent you a room. And that's why you live here. For now, anyway. Until you find another place."

She wrinkled her nose in confusion.

"Don't know what you mean."

"Let's practice the story so it seems natural. Like we're not lying."

"Yer the boss."

They spent nearly forty-five minutes rehearsing the outlines of the story so that both could recite it on demand.

Afterward, Phillip got up from the table and stretched his arms. He looked outside and the sun was already dropping behind the trees as autumn settled in.

"My sister invited me to dinner at her place tonight," he said. "I'm going to leave you by yourself. How does that sound?"

"Yer the boss."

"Are you going to be comfortable being alone? You can't go outside. I haven't told my neighbors about you. Besides, I have no idea what you would do or say around them."

"I like people."

"I'm sure you do. But you say strange things. And you're, well, different. You might frighten some people. For instance, we wear clothes. You can't go walking around naked. You could get arrested. They might think you're on drugs."

She shrugged and twisted her mouth in apparent confusion.

"I like no clothes."

"You *have* to wear clothes Sofia."

"Yer the boss."

"Tell me something," Phillip said. "It's been bugging me. The more we talk, the more your vocabulary grows. And you have a funny accent. Sometimes you sound like you're from Ireland, then other times like you're from France. And yet, every now and then you have another strange accent. Where did you learn to talk?"

"I talk like people who find me. I'll talk like you soon."

"You're very strange," he said.

"You like me?"

"I'm not sure."

"You're a mean boss," she pouted.

15

Phillip took a shower and was forced to lock the door from the inside to keep Sofia out.

"Why can't I come in?"

"It's private. This is how I like it."

"You're funny," she said, sitting on the floor outside the bathroom.

When he finished and came outside, he nearly tripped over her. He recovered and stepped over her as if she were a traffic cone. She followed him into the bedroom and sat on the bed watching him.

"Do you have to do that?" he said, standing in his underwear.

"Do what, *Fillleeeep*?"

"Watch me get dressed."

"I like watching you."

"Mmm," he said, turning to pick out a pair of slacks

from his closet. He grabbed a shirt and a fleece vest. He finished dressing, without talking to her. She simply watched.

"Can I go with you?"

"No."

"Why not?"

"You wouldn't like it. And you would do something to embarrass me."

"Do you like me, *Fillleeeep*?"

He looked at her and saw a smidgen of fragility he had not noticed earlier.

"Of course, I like you."

"I think you mad at me."

"I'm not angry. I'm just a little confused."

"I don't want you be angry. Don't be a mean boss."

"I'm not angry, I promise."

"Not my fault left out of the water too long."

"I don't want to talk about it. Come with me."

He walked down the hallway through the kitchen and into the family room.

"Sit here," he said patting the couch seat next to him.

She sat with her hands in her lap.

"When I'm gone, I think you should watch some TV and just sit here. I'll only be gone for about an hour and a half."

She smiled. "Yer the boss."

"So, I'm going to show you quickly how to watch TV and to change channels. My guess — and this is just a wild guess — you don't know what a TV is."

She shrugged.

He picked up the cable remote and explained what

he was going to do and how there would be sounds and pictures coming from the large flat-screen TV in front of them.

"Are you ready?"

"Yes."

He pushed the button, and the screen came alive with a news broadcast. Her green eyes grew large as she processed the sounds and pictures.

She looked at him in alarm, then back at the TV, then back at him.

"*Fillleeeep,*" she said.

"Yes?"

"*Fillleeeep.* What is it?"

"These are just shows that portray the world. Don't be afraid of them. They're not actually in the room with us. It's like a reflection of people, who are someplace else. Does that make sense?"

"No. Don't like it. They are flat."

"That's the reflection, like on the surface of calm water."

Phillip showed her how to change the channels, then put the controller in her hand. She dropped it on the floor.

He picked it up and put it in her palm, keeping his hand around her hand. He forced her to press the up and down arrows to change stations. After fifteen minutes he stood.

"I have to leave now. I'll be back in a while. You watch TV."

She sat mesmerized in front of the television, methodically going through every channel, her eyes very wide.

"Sofia, look at me."

She looked up.

"Promise me that you'll not go outside. And that you'll stay here in this room and watch TV."

She didn't answer and turned back to look at the TV.

He sighed, went to the kitchen, grabbed his keys, and entered the garage.

16

"You look a little pale today," Felicia said, sitting across from him at the dining room table.

"No he doesn't," Ernie said. "Leave the poor guy alone."

Felicia was Phillip's only sibling. She was forty-two years old and lived in the same seaside town. She owned a small gift shop in the downtown section. Her husband Ernie was a real estate lawyer. They lived in the fancy part of town and had a large home with a view of the ocean.

"So, have you heard any more about the promotion?" Felicia said. "Has your boss said anything?"

"Well," Phillip said, "I've been at the branch the longest, and I'm the assistant branch manager. I can't believe they won't offer me the new branch in the next town. I mean, Mr. Sampson has said as much."

"That would be a great promotion for you," Ernie said, taking a sip of wine. "You deserve it. Nice raise I bet. And a chance to reset things." He exchanged glances with Felicia.

"Have you thought about dating?" Felicia said quickly, almost devouring the words along with a mouthful of roasted cod.

"No, haven't really thought of it. It's been nine or ten months since the divorce. I'll get around to it."

"It's been a year and two months, actually," she said.

"Whatever," Phillip said. "I'll get around to dating soon enough. Work has been a bear. And I still have the stupid boat in the water. I forgot to get it hauled this year."

The sudden thought of the boat and the day's events sent a frisson of anxiety across Phillip's chest.

"You should sell that boat," Ernie said. "Best thing I ever did was sell the Grady White. You don't need a boat. You need to have friends who have boats." He laughed.

"I didn't want the darn thing in the first place," Phillip said. "It was her idea."

Felicia smiled. "Well, sell it then. Case closed."

They had desert then sat and watched a news broadcast that was focused on the effects of the recent nor'easter.

"We lost power for two hours," Felicia said.

"Our neighborhood was lucky," Phillip said, looking at his watch. "You know, I really should get going."

"What's the rush?" Felicia said. "Tomorrow's Sunday. Your day off. Relax tonight."

"No really. I'm a little tired. I need to get home.

"What's the rush?" Ernie said. "Have another drink."

"I really need to get going," Phillip said.

_17_

The garage door groaned as it closed behind him. Phillip had long thought of garage doors as modern-day drawbridges, folding up and down to protect the homeowner from the outside world. Or so it seemed.

The outside world had been a challenge for Phillip. He was an average man destined and restricted to the middle. He was of average height and weight. He was not attractive nor unattractive. He was thoughtful, kind, and avoided conflict with something approaching passion. His voice was calm and carried the slightest intonation of reserve.

Mr. Dibbs, his high school guidance counselor, once told Phillip that average students like him did not get enough attention. "If you have ADHD, or were a child prodigy or the starting quarterback, you'd get plenty of attention. But people in the middle just slide by with scant notice." Phillip had a feeling that Mr. Dibbs, a sad, small man, was talking about himself. But as the years went by, Phillip realized he was indeed talking about him.

Phillip sat inside his car in the garage with the engine off. He glanced once or twice at the kitchen door. The lights were on inside. He could faintly hear the TV.

It was a difficult ending to a difficult day. Inside his house, there was either a woman watching TV, or there was no one inside watching TV. Both options presented their own problems. If the woman was there, it would confirm that something very strange and inexplicable had happened to him that day and would require some psychic reconciliation. And if no one was there, he needed to confront the fact that he was not well.

When his former wife Martha had sat down with him one evening after dinner and said she was leaving him, he was struck by the same overwhelming feeling of strangeness. Martha talked that evening about how she and Warren—Phillip's best friend—had fallen in love. It was unexpected and not planned, she said.

Phillip listened, his hands in his lap, much as he had sat with Mr. Dibbs many years before. When Martha was finished, Phillip did not know what to do.

"Did you hear anything I just said?" Martha asked him.

"Yes."

"Well, say something," she prodded him.

"I don't know what to say," he said.

"Tell me you're angry. Tell me you hate Warren."

"I don't hate Warren," he said.

"Oh God, Phil," she said, "you should show a little passion every now and then."

Staring at the cold steering wheel in the garage, Phillip felt scared, just like he did that night with Martha.

He opened the car door, closed it, and walked to the kitchen door. The TV could be heard blaring.

18

The kitchen table was covered with items from the refrigerator including a milk container, an orange juice container, an opened jar of blueberry jam, a bag of carrots that was torn open. A half-eaten stalk of celery was on the floor, next to several whole onions that appeared to have been thrown there. A carton of eggs had been dropped onto the floor. Several eggs had broken, and their yellow yolks had oozed onto the floor.

The refrigerator door was open and had probably been open for a while since its little compressor was furiously pounding away.

He turned to look in the family room.

Sofia lay across the couch, her eyes closed and her mouth partly open. In front of her on the small table was an assortment of food items including open cracker boxes and a dented can of tomato sauce that she apparently was not able to open.

There were also two opened cans of beer. He lifted one of the cans and it was empty; the second one was empty as well. So was a can of Diet Coke.

The TV channel was set to a Spanish language crime show. He found the remote and turned off the TV.

"Sofia," he said, shaking her shoulder. She did not respond.

He sighed and sat at the small, upholstered chair next to the couch and surveyed the room, the kitchen behind him, and the reclining body of the strange woman from the ocean.

"Sofia," he said again, this time much louder. She didn't respond.

At least she's still wearing clothes.

He yawned violently and realized how tired he was. He stood, walked over, and picked up Sofia, who remained inert.

Phillip took her down the hall to the spare bedroom, took off her shoes and socks, and put her under the sheets fully clad. He turned off the bedside light and closed her door.

It took him nearly an hour to clean up the house. He mopped the kitchen floor and finally surrendered to the comfort of his bed wearing a tee shirt and his long pajama bottoms. He did not remember turning off the light.

He was sound asleep, dreaming an indistinct story involving a bank building and a fire truck when he felt someone touch him.

"Hey!" he said startled and sitting up in the dark.

"Fillleeeep," she said. "Help me."

19

He turned on the bedside light. She was kneeling next to him with her elbows on the bed.

"What's wrong, Sofia."

"My body feels bad," she said.

Phillip tried to rid his brain of the sleep chemicals by shaking it, then he focused on her face in the glare of the light.

She looked pale and her eyes were no longer piercing; they were pleading.

"Help me," she said, putting her cold left hand on his wrist.

"What's wrong with you?"

She shrugged. "Don't know."

"Are you in pain?"

"Maybe."

"Sofia, I'm trying to help but I don't know what's wrong. Is it your stomach? Your head?"

"Maybe my head."

He reached over and felt her forehead; it was normal. He leaned forward and looked at her eyes. They were bloodshot. He could smell beer on her breath.

"I think you have a hangover," he said.

"I'm going to die," she said.

"You're not going to die. Just go back to bed. You'll be fine in the morning."

"I don't like this feeling."

"No one does," he said. "Please. Just go back to bed."

She stood, walked around the bed, and got under the covers.

"Hey, you can't do that," he said sitting up. "Out. Go to your own bed."

"Why can't I stay here?"

"This is my bed. It's just for me. You have your own bed."

She slid over and wrapped her arms around his chest, putting her head against his shoulder.

He pried her arms off, rolled out of bed, and walked around to her side of the bed.

"Come," he said holding out his hand.

"I like this bed."

"Come," he said reaching down and grabbing her hand. He pulled her up and led her across the hall to her bed. He tucked her in.

"Good night," he said. "You'll feel better in the morning."

"You're mean," she said.

"You need to sleep."

"You're a mean boss."

20

Phillip woke to the strange sounds of crunching as if some-one were walking on broken shards of glass.

He opened his eyes and saw Sofia sitting on the floor three feet away with her back against the wall. She had a stalk of celery in her right hand and the salt shaker in her left.

"You make funny noise when you sleep," she said.

He blinked several times.

"I don't make funny noises," he said, though Martha had complained of the same nocturnal phenomena.

"I think you were crying."

"I wasn't crying. Why would I cry?"

"Don't know. Are you sad?"

Phillip closed his eyes again and left them closed for a long time.

"Hey," she poked him with the celery. "My head hurts. And I forgot about the body thing that I have to do."

His eyelids flew open.

"What body thing?"

"You know."

"No I don't."

"The thing where you empty your body."

He sat up. "Did you empty your body in your bed?"

"No. I wanted to, but I knew you would be mad. Don't you have a little house outside? Show me."

Phillip jumped out of bed, pulled her up off the floor, and led her to the bathroom. He showed her how the toilet worked and flushed it once as an example.

She kneeled and put her hands in water as it filled back up.

"Oh god, please don't do that Sofia," he said, pulling her up and taking her to the sink to wash her hands. "Never—let me repeat—never put your hands in the toilet. There are germs and unsafe things in there. Just do your business, wipe yourself and flush."

"Wipe? What is that?"

This can't be happening.

Phillip had her wash her hands, dried them with a hand towel, then took her to the toilet again. He showed her the roll of toilet paper, demonstrated how to pull a bunch of it, then struggled with how to show her the rest.

"Um, well you—you know, you wipe yourself to stay clean, and you, you know, throw the used tissues into the toilet when you're finished. You stand up and you flush."

Sofia unbuttoned her slacks, pulled down the zipper, and started to pull down her white cotton jockey underwear.

"Hey," he said. "You do that privately."

"Why?" she said, pulling the underwear down and sitting on the toilet.

He raced out of the room and closed the door.

"Keep the door closed when you do that," he said loudly.

"Yer the boss."

21

Phillip went into the kitchen, ground some coffee beans, and started up the coffee machine. The smell of freshly brewed coffee always made him feel good and he momentarily forgot he had a house guest.

The flushing toilet returned his attention to the recurring disturbance of the visitor. He heard her walking down the hallway to the kitchen and he reached into a cupboard and pulled out a box of cereal. From another cupboard, he took out a small white bowl, grabbed a spoon from the drawer, and put those items onto the kitchen table.

Phillip looked up and saw her standing in the kitchen staring at the box of cereal.

"What is that?" she said.

"Food."

"Can I have?"

"Of course. Sit down." He pointed to a chair.

As she started to sit, he said, "Oh, for heaven's sake Sofia!"

She looked confused.

"What is that?" he said pointing at the hallway floor.

Sofia turned around. A long white trail of toilet paper ran from the back of her slacks to the bathroom.

"Oh," she said, pulling the end of the paper out. "I guess it follow me." She dropped the ribbon of paper and it floated slowly down to the floor.

He went over and picked up the end of the toilet paper.

"We usually leave this on the roll," he said, picking up the long single strand as he followed it down the hallway. In the bathroom, he compacted the toilet paper into a single ball and pushed it into the waste basket.

When he returned to the kitchen, she was sitting at the table shaking the box of cereal.

"What is it?" she said, sniffing the box.

"Food. Let's see if you like it."

He grabbed the milk from the refrigerator, another bowl and spoon, and poured cereal and milk into two bowls. He showed her how to eat it.

She took a small mouthful and slowly chewed it, staring at him all the time. She finally swallowed.

"Do you like it?"

"Maybe."

"Try some more." He commenced eating his cereal. She followed along, carefully examining each spoonful of milk and cereal before she put it in her mouth.

When they finished, he said, "Would you like some coffee?"

"I don't know."

He pulled two mugs from a cupboard, poured coffee into both, and put them on the table. He grabbed the sugar bowl, a spoon, and the milk from the refrigerator. He put two heaping spoonfuls of sugar into a mug and poured some milk, stirring all the time. He pushed it over to her. He drank his black.

"What is that?" she said pointing to the sugar bowl.

"Sugar. It's sweet. Have you had sugar before?"

"Maybe."

"The coffee is hot so be careful." He took a sip of his.

She lifted the cup, smelled it, and made a small grimace, then took the tiniest of sips.

"I don't like it," she said.

"Try another sip," he said.

She tried another one and swallowed it slowly, her Adam's apple moving up and down.

"Maybe I like it." When he took a sip, she also took one. They sat in silence, sipping.

"Yesterday was a strange day," he said.

She shrugged.

"I'm not sure what to do with you," he said.

"Yer the boss."

"Yes, you keep saying that," Phillip said, "but it doesn't really help me. I would have a hard time getting anyone to believe what happened yesterday. They would think I was crazy."

"Crazy?"

He raised his right hand next to his temple and used his forefinger to rotate it in a circle.

"Oh, that," she made a guttural laugh, throwing her head back. "Yes, you are crazy."

"Don't say that."

"If you say so."

He paused and twisted his mouth in concentration.

"No one will believe how you came onto my boat. And then changed into another thing. And are here now."

"So?" she said finishing her coffee. She pulled the sugar bowl toward her and poked her finger into the thick white crystals. She put her finger in her mouth.

"Mmm," she said. "Can I have more?"

"I suppose," he said standing to get the coffee pot.

She picked up the sugar bowl and poured it into her open mouth, the crystals sweeping onto her shirt and the table top.

He returned with the coffee pot.

"Sofia! Why do you do things like that?" he said.

"You said I could have more," she said defiantly. "Don't be an angry boss."

"I meant you could put more of it in your coffee."

"I like sugar," she said, working her mouth in an exaggerated chewing motion as she crunched and swallowed through the mass of sugar. Stray crystals stuck to her chin and the corners of her mouth leaving her with a thin white mustache.

He took the bowl back from her, putting two spoonfuls into her mug along with milk and fresh coffee.

She drank it faster this time and was through her cup before he had taken a second sip.

"That's too fast," he said. "You should try to drink it slower."

"You should drink faster."

He sighed and drank in silence.

"You're using more words now," he said. "Why is that? You could barely speak English before."

She shrugged.

"When do I do my work? Do you have nets to mend?"

"I don't have nets," he said. "You don't have to work."

"I don't?"

"No."

"Aren't you the boss?"

"No. I'm the person who found you."

"Then you are the boss."

"I'm not your boss."

"If you found me, then you are the boss."

He was no longer disturbed by her piercing green eyes, and he stared for a while at her face. "Today's Sunday," he said finally as if it were the conclusion of a lengthy discussion.

"What is that?"

"I'm off work today. I usually go to the pub to watch the football game with my friends."

"I don't know what you are talking about."

"No, I guessed as much. But I have a problem. When I left you in front of the TV yesterday, I came back and the house was a mess. And you were passed out on the couch."

She shrugged.

"So, I can't leave you alone. And I can't take you with me to the pub."

"Take me to the pub. I think I know that place."

"You do?"

"Yes. People drinking bubbly stuff as you have. And talking. And laughing. And spitting into little buckets. I like that."

"I can't take you there. It would be a disaster. And we don't have buckets to spit into anymore."

Phillip's strength was his proclivity to problem solve when confronted with a disturbance. It distracted him and of course, if one solves a problem, the problems go away.

"*Fillleeeep,*" she said reaching across the table and putting her hands above and below his right hand, "please take me to the pub with you. I really want to go."

He was not aware at that moment that the relationship had changed. With a pleading voice, a mischievous pouting face, and the pressing of her warm, soft hands around his, Sofia altered the balance of power between them.

22

Phillip ignored Sofia's distress about the speed of the vehicle, the sounds it made, and the stop-and-go lurching.

"Oooh," she yelled at one point. "Phillip you will make a mess."

"Now you're the baby," he said. It felt good to push back.

They had rehearsed the story about how they met. It went like this: Phillip's sister had mentioned she knew Sofia, a young person who was looking to rent a room. She recommended Phillip and, *voila*, Sofia was renting a room from him. The fact that Phillip had not shared these details with his sister did not bother him; even though it was a small town, their social circles were amazingly separate swirling galaxies rarely intersecting.

Phillip told Sofia that she could not drink beer at the pub. Nor could she "empty her body" while she was there. He had no idea how she would navigate a bathroom stall with other women around, and the thought of her doing something bizarre pained him.

Of equal concern, though, was that his former wife and new husband would be there. Phillip enjoyed hanging out with the rag-tag group of locals at the pub for football games. He was on the shy side of the spectrum of social interaction, but this group of mostly young men and women accepted him for who he was: a slightly reticent, somewhat boring, assistant bank manager who never drank too much or made a scene.

His extraordinary calm was in full demonstration when he hardly made a fuss about the unseemly act of his best friend stealing his wife.

Phillip sometimes wondered whether his friends pitied him. But that was a small matter. He could adapt to every single obstacle life presented.

"Remember, you're from Wisconsin," he said as they walked along the sidewalk to the pub. "Can you say it, please?"

"Whisshconsin."

"Close enough. OK, and if someone asks you what town in Wisconsin, you say, 'I don't want to talk about my small town.'"

"Yer the boss."

"And no beer. And no trips to the bathroom."

"*Fillleeeep* you are funny."

"Promise me you won't drink beer or go to the bathroom."

"What does 'promise' mean?"

"It means you won't do those things."

"You are funny."

It was 3 p.m. when they entered the pub since it was a 4 p.m. game. The pub was not large, with a semi-circular bar in the front with several TV sets on the surrounding walls. Farther back was a larger TV set with tables in front.

Phillip made his way to a group of people who sat in front of the big TV set.

"Hey Phil," said a short, bearded man with a sun-faded baseball cap. "Who you got with ya?"

The group of seven turned to look. Strangers are always a curiosity to small-town folk.

"Hey Phil," said Cathy, one of his oldest friends. She was tall, lanky, and wore her long sandy blonde hair in a pony tail. "Who's your friend?"

"This is Sofia," he said. "She's renting a room at my place. Thought I'd introduce her to some of the local, um, hoodlums."

Phillip was not known to make jokes and the fact that he did—and got a good laugh in the process—spiked everyone's attention.

And there was Sofia of course.

Phillip had forgotten that her unusual personality and attractiveness had a propensity to disrupt. She had certainly altered his personal trajectory.

Bill Stephenson was a hardworking carpenter with large shoulders and arms. He worked out daily in a local gym and his neck seemed unnecessarily thick to sustain his smallish head. Bill sported a small tattoo of a star on the right side of his neck under his ear.

"Well, hello Sofia," Bill said standing up and shaking

her hand. Phillip noted that no one in the group customarily stood up to greet new attendees, and it was yet another small alarm bell warning of Sofia's effect on people.

Two other men stood to introduce themselves to Sofia, which again was not normal.

Phillip scanned the group and noticed that Martha and Warren were not in attendance.

Thank god they're not here.

Several chairs were brought over to add to the group and a waitress stopped by. Phillip ordered two Diet Cokes.

"Not drinking today?" Cathy said, sitting on Phillip's right side.

"Naw. Was at my sister's for dinner last night. Enough booze for me for a while."

"Well, you barely drink anyway, Phil," she laughed.

She leaned in and whispered to him. "So where did you get her from? I have to say she's the best-looking Russian mail-order bride I've ever seen. I think Bill will need a drool bucket soon."

"It's not like that, Cathy. You of all people know that's not my style."

"Well, after Martha and Warren's wedding, you'd be excused for getting a little whacky," she said.

"I don't feel like talking about them today," he said, a wan smile crossing his face.

Sofia sat on Phillip's left, and next to Bill. Across from her sat Susanne, who worked at the pub but was off on Sundays.

Phillip's ears perked up when he heard Susanne mention Wisconsin.

"Oh, it's a small town but I don't want to talk about it."

"Are you on the lam for robbing a bank?" Bill asked.

Sofia turned to look at Phillip, looking for guidance.

"Hey," Phillip said, "cut the poor woman some slack. She left her town to get away from it and experience the rest of the country."

"She sounds like she's from Poland or something," Cathy said over Phillip's shoulder.

"I like Poland," Sofia said.

"You've been to Poland?" Bill asked.

"Yes."

"What were you doing there?" he said, taking a big sip of beer.

"Like always. Work, work, work."

"What kind of work?" Cathy asked.

"Hey, people, we just got here," Phillip said. "Can't we just relax for a few minutes?"

There was a commotion behind the group, then Phillip heard Martha and her signature greeting, "Wazzup!"

23

There are many strange social behaviors in a small town that would not work in other settings. A compact circle of residents must live together in peace and harmony. As a result, some uncomfortable things are simply taken for granted and absorbed into everyday life.

For instance, there was the unfortunate affair between Martha and Warren. The affair was widely known amongst the small group. All, that is, except Phillip.

Everyone kept the secret until Martha finally asked for a divorce. Phillip guessed at that point that everyone had known all along.

Remarkably, during the divorce and the new marriage afterward, the group socialized as if nothing had changed. The awkwardness that might accompany social engagements never occurred. It was as if Phillip and Martha had never been married for five years.

"Hey Phil," Warren said, slapping him on the shoulder. Warren was a long-time shoulder slapper. Phillip found it a condescending behavior. "How ya doing, pardner."

Warren also affected a fake cowboy accent from time to time.

"Fine, thanks," Phillip said. "How are things with you?"

"Mighty fine. Mighty fine, thank you."

"How's the banking business these days?"

"It's still there," Phillip said. "I'm hoping to get promoted to manage the new branch opening soon."

"Well, you always were the ambitious one, that's for sure."

"How's the concrete pouring business?" Phillip asked

"Fine. Mighty fine, pardner. Hey, who's that chick? Where she'd come from?"

"Oh, that's Sofia."

"Well, she is one smoking beauty, that's for sure. Bill drag her here?"

"No. She's with me."

Warren dropped his hand off Phillip's shoulder and stood back a step to look at him.

"She's with you?"

"Yes. She's renting a room at the house. I've got a lot of space these days."

"Why you old dog, you! I bet she's *renting a room* from ya, pardner." Warren used air quotes for emphasis.

"It's not like that, Warren."

"Sure, pardner. You going to introduce me?"

"No. I think you can manage that on your own." But Warren was already walking toward Sofia who was engrossed in conversation.

Cathy stood up.

"Hey, keep me company for a smoke outside," she said to Phillip.

"Sure," he said, glancing nervously at Sofia.

They stood outside in the chilly October air while she puffed furiously on her cigarette.

"So where did you meet her?"

"Sofia?"

"No, Mother Theresa. Of course, Sofia."

"I already told folks inside. My sister said she was looking for a room to rent. That's it."

"That's it?"

"That's it."

She took a long pull on the cigarette and blew it out the side of her mouth, pursing her lips to do so.

"I don't know, Phil. We've known each other for a long time. Since elementary school. Something doesn't add up if you know what I mean."

"Cathy, she's renting a room from me. I'm hoping she'll find another place soon. You have any ideas where she could find a room to rent here?"

"Mmm," she said taking another drag. "I hate to say this, but maybe the divorce was kind of tough on you. We never talked about it."

"You never asked."

"That's true. I thought it would be impolite."

He shrugged.

Phillip was not a shrugger, *per se*. Since Sofia had splashed into his life, he noticed that she would simply shrug if she either didn't know how to respond or didn't want to respond. He liked the compact, simple gesture and was eager to incorporate it into his repertoire.

Cathy squinted at him, puffing on the cigarette.

"What?" he said.

"Nothing."

"I'm cold," he said. "I'm going in."

"I'll be in after I finish this stupid cancer stick."

"You should really stop smoking."

"You should really stop lying about Sofia."

Phillip had walked a mere five steps into the pub when he ran headlong into Martha.

"Come here," she hissed, pulling his jacket sleeve, and stepping into the small hallway leading to the kitchen area. Martha was a jacket and sleeve puller; she did not like touching skin and preferred the safety of cloth to direct human contact.

"I can't believe you had the *gall*," she said, her hazel eyes blazing and her eyelashes blinking like an epileptic semaphore.

"What are you talking about Martha?"

"Don't play stupid with me, Phil. You know *exactly* what I mean."

"Sorry, I don't. I need to get going if you don't mind."

"Oh, you mean to gather up your little tart and retreat to your love nest?"

"I see. You're talking about Sofia."

"Are those *my* clothes she's wearing?"

"You left those behind, remember? You told me to throw them away."

"How could you bring her *here*? In *my* clothes. These are *my* friends, for god's sake."

Standing in the confined space, with the dim lighting and the smell of beer and fried food, Phillip experienced a tiny shudder of revulsion.

She really is a bitch. Felicia told me a hundred times and I couldn't see it. Funny.

"Take a deep breath, Martha. Go have a glass of chardonnay. You'll be fine."

He walked back into the pub and discovered Sofia was holding court. His palms dampened, and he rushed over, pushing aside several people.

"Hey Sofia, we really have to get going," he said.

She looked up from her chair. She had an empty wine glass in her hand.

"The game just started," Bill said. "Sit down and chill."

Normally, in days past, Phillip would sit down when directed and chill.

"No, come on Sofia. Please."

"Oh, must we go?" she said, putting her glass on the table.

Warren and Bill combined to pester Phillip into staying longer, but to no avail.

Halfway to the front door, he heard Warren say from behind, "Mama mia!"

Followed immediately by Martha saying, "Shut up, Warren."

"You promised me you wouldn't drink alcohol," he said in the car.

"You said beer."

"I did say beer, but I meant all kinds of alcohol. Alcohol of any variety is the issue."

"Yer the boss."

They drove in silence as he processed his interaction with Martha.

She said I had the gall? Me? She's a witch. And a bitch.

He smiled; he had never made a joke to himself before.

"I like your friends," she said.

"They're all right, I guess. By the way, who bought you the glass of wine?"

"Bill. The one with the star on his neck. Why does he have a star on his neck?"

"He told me once, but I forget. Something about his

'north star.'"

"He is like all the other men," she laughed. "Always the same. Except you *Fillleeeep*. You are different."

"Now you have a Polish accent. Have you been to Poland?"

She shrugged.

"Did Bill just buy you that glass of wine without asking?"

"Yes. He put it in front of me. I liked it. Very good. But it makes my head dizzy."

"He's a character."

"Yes. He wanted to do the in-out thing. He looks very strong."

"What!"

She looked at him in alarm.

"What is wrong?"

"Bill wanted to do what?"

"The in-out thing. You know."

"How do you know? What did he say to you?"

"Oh, you can tell. I can see it. Men."

"That's silly, Sofia. You can't tell by just looking."

"Not just looking." She reached her left hand across the center console and squeezed his right thigh.

"What are you doing?"

"That's what Bill did. Very fast. When I reached for the wine. He's funny."

"He what!" Phillip said. "That son of a—"

"Why are you shouting now? I don't like it when you shout. Don't be an angry boss."

"That's just plain rude and insulting. What an idiot."

"I like Bill. I like his star."

"He's an idiot."

"If you say so. I have to empty my body."

"Don't do it here."

"Hurry *Fillleeeep*," she laughed. "You worry so much."

"What a jerk that man is!"

26

Phillip was still angry about Bill's open flirtation at the pub. He conceded that Sofia had been introduced as a person renting a room from Phillip so that it was possible Bill saw nothing inappropriate about hitting on her.

The more Phillip thought about it, the more confused he got. Was he offended? If so, why? Sofia was not his girl-friend. But did Bill know that from the brief meeting?

Phillip was distracted when they got home, and he could barely pay attention to the football game on TV.

"Why are they doing that?" Sofia asked while watching the game.

"Doing what?" he said.

"You know. Hitting each other. Why must they wear things to make themselves look bigger. Is that to scare someone?"

"Yes. They want to scare people."

Bill is such a jerk.

"Can we look at the other things? I like the other things."

"I can't watch cartoons now."

"Is that what you call them?"

"Yes, you like cartoons. Actually, I don't care. Let's watch cartoons."

He changed the channel and found reruns of South Park.

"They have funny bodies. And funny voices."

"I'm going to order pizza. Do you like pizza?"

She shrugged. "Is it green?"

"No, it's red and white."

She frowned. Phillip noticed that the sight and smell of any type of meat or fish product sent shivers through Sofia.

"I'm going to get it delivered. I'm frightened of leaving you alone. You're like a child."

"I'm not a child," she said.

"I said you're *like* a child. You most certainly are *not* a child. Just ask Bill."

"I like Bill."

"Mmm."

Later that evening, after finishing the pizza and Diet Cokes, Phillip looked at Sofia across the table, the pizza box between them.

"Tomorrow I have to go to work."

"Work, work, work."

"Yes, but I have to leave you here. Alone. I don't have anyone to babysit you."

"I'm not a baby."

"But you're capable of mischief, Sofia."

"I don't know that word."

"It means trouble. You are capable of creating trouble."

"I like pizzz," she said, pointing at the greasy box.

"Pizza. It's called pizza. I'm glad you liked it. Now about tomorrow."

"Will you get more pizza for tomorrow?"

"I suppose."

"With coffee and sugar and milk?"

"No, that's for mornings."

"I like the red and white pizza."

"So, about tomorrow. There's no beer in the house, so you can't get in trouble there. But you have to promise you'll stay inside the house all day."

"OK."

"I'm going to bed now. You can stay up and watch cartoons or anything for that matter. Or go to bed."

"Can I sleep in your bed tonight? I don't like it by myself. It's not good, *Fillleeeep*. It makes me feel funny."

"No, Sofia. We've been over this before. You sleep in your bed, and I sleep in mine."

"We don't have to do the in-out thing."

He blushed and then was embarrassed that he blushed. "Enough with the in-out thing. Can't two adults just have a friendly relationship without the in-out thing?"

"You don't like the in-out thing?"

"Oh, for god's sake," he said standing. He put the empty pizza box next to the trash can. "Good night. I'll see you in the morning."

As he was walking down the hallway, she yelled to him, "*Fillleeeep*, do I still need to do the thing with my mouth?

I don't like it."

He stopped. "Yes, Sophia. Brush your teeth at night and in the morning. And don't swallow the toothpaste. You spit it out. Then rinse. You're not supposed to eat it."

"I don't like it."

"I'm the boss."

Why the hell did I say that?

27

He woke to the sound of laughter. His clock radio showed 2:42 a.m.

Phillip sat up and listened. The laughter was coming from the TV set in the living room. He stood, opened his door into the fully lit house, and squinted in the glare. Sofia's room was open, and he could see she was not in bed.

He walked down the hallway. The TV was on showing an old episode of the Mary Tyler Moore Show.

"Oh lord," he said out loud.

Sofia was lying on the couch, her face hidden by her disheveled mop of hair. She was also naked, except for his white jockey underwear.

He walked over and picked up the TV controller and turned it off. Her clothes were thrown on the floor.

Phillip sat down and shook her arm. She was breathing heavily and did not wake.

He shook her harder. "Sofia, wake up. SOFIA!"

She roused and then sat up on her elbow.

"Who are you?"

"It's me Sofia. Phillip."

"Oh. The boss."

"You need to go to bed."

She dropped her head onto the couch and closed her eyes. He stared at her.

"Sofia."

She didn't move.

"Why do you keep taking off your clothes?"

She didn't answer.

Just leave her here.

He stood up and yawned. Then he sighed, reached down, and picked her up in his arms.

Damn, she's heavy.

He carried her down the hallway, put her into her bed, turned off the light, and closed the door. Phillip returned to the living room, picked up her clothes, tidied up a couple of items including a nearly full can of Diet Coke, and an issue of *National Geographic* that was open to a story on grasshoppers.

He turned off the lights and went to bed.

His alarm went off at seven in the morning and he lay on his side staring at the clock radio's numbers until they showed 7:07.

He got up and opened Sofia's door. She was still in bed. He quickly took his shower and was nearly done when he heard the bathroom door open.

"Hey!" he said.

"What are you doing?" Sofia said.

"I'm taking a shower. You shouldn't come in when someone's taking a shower Sofia."

"I like the rain-thing."

The shower curtain pulled back and Sofia stood there naked except for his white jockey underwear.

"Hey!" he yelled, closing the curtain.

She pulled it open again and looked at him.

"Can I do the rain thing with you?"

"For God's sakes, Sofia," he said pulling the curtain closed yet again. "No. Please let me shower alone. I'll have breakfast for you in a minute."

"Angry boss," she said, sitting on the toilet. "I have to empty myself."

"Just hurry," he said. "You have to learn to respect people's privacy, Sofia."

"I don't know what you mean," she said yawning. She used the toilet paper and flushed when she was done.

She pulled the curtain back again.

This time he turned his back to her and yelled "Sofia, stop it!"

"You have fur on your back."

"Go!" he yelled.

She pulled the curtain back and left.

29

They had cereal again for breakfast, but Phillip kept the sugar bowl close to him. Once when he stood to get the coffee pot, she put her hand in the bowl and stuffed the sugar into her mouth before he sat back down. White crystals littered the tabletop and stuck to her chin. She avoided looking at him.

"Don't do that Sofia."

"OK."

They ate in silence. When they were finished, he took the empty bowls and spoons to the sink, along with the sugar bowl.

"Mean boss," she said under her breath.

He sat back down, looked at his watch, and said, "Sofia, you promise to stay inside the house today, correct?"

"If you say so."

"I say so."

She shrugged.

"But I'm going to try something. It will help me to stay in contact with you."

She frowned and pinched her lips in confusion.

Phillip took his cell phone out of his back pocket and put it on the table.

"Sofia, this is my phone that I carry with me all the time."

"It has lights on it."

"Yes, it has lights on it. But it's also a telephone. And I'm going to call you today and I need you to answer the phone to talk to me. How does that sound?"

She shrugged.

"OK. So let's do a quick practice run."

"Run? You want me to run?"

"No. Let's practice something." He stood up and went to the wall phone next to the kitchen door. He picked up the receiver and held it against his ear, spoke several words as a demonstration into the mouthpiece, and then hung it up.

"I'm going to call you today at noon and this phone is going to ring. It has bells inside. It makes a noise when someone calls. You pick it up and talk to me, OK?"

She shook her head. "No."

"What do you mean 'no?' Please come here."

"No."

"Sofia, this is not going to hurt you. Please come here."

"No. I don't like it."

Because Phillip was pressed for time, he moved into problem-solving mode. "I'm the boss. Come here, please."

She stood and came to the phone. He made her pick it up and showed her how to listen and speak.

"I don't like it," she repeated.

"Now, I'm going to use my cell phone here, and I'm going to call this other phone. It's going to ring and make a noise. Then you pick up the phone and talk to me. When we're done you put the phone back.

She eyed him nervously, her eyes narrowed.

He dialed his home number, and the wall phone came to life with a series of rings. Sofia jumped, her eyes wide and fitful. She stood back from the phone and covered her ears with her hands.

"Pick it up," he said.

"No."

He went over and picked up the phone and handed it to her. Sofia held it at arm's length and grimaced.

"Put to your ear."

She timorously put it against her ear, as if it were a dangerous animal.

Phillip turned his back and spoke into his phone. "Can you hear me?"

"Who are you?" she said into the phone.

He turned to face her and spoke both into his phone and to her at the same time.

"It's me," he said. "I'm calling you."

She dropped the phone onto the floor and stood back.

"Fine," he said, picking up the phone by its cord. "Never mind."

He looked at his watch again.

"You can't go outside. You can't eat sugar. You can't

do anything except watch TV and eat green things in the refrigerator."

She shrugged.

I'll wake up from this, sooner or later. This is very strange.

30

Phillip unlocked the bank's front door, relocked it behind him, and turned off the alarm. He made a cup of coffee for himself using the single-serve machine in the small kitchen. Typically, he arrived at the bank thirty minutes before it opened for business. This gave him time to make sure the tellers' money drawers were full and accounted for, the employee timecards were in order, and that the bank was running smoothly when Mr. Sampson arrived later in the morning.

Mr. Sampson rarely arrived before ten o'clock, which was an hour after the bank opened. Phillip knew some of the tellers disapproved of Mr. Sampson's tardiness, but he chose to avoid confronting them. Besides, the head teller Sally Jennings was their direct manager and he let her manage the staff herself.

Within the small ecosystem of the branch bank, Phillip

took pride in being the serious, no-nonsense assistant manager who kept the trains running on time. Mr. Sampson, by contrast, was gregarious and perhaps a bit sloppy by Phillip's standards.

Sally, a divorced single mother, was a strict taskmaster with her tellers. But Mr. Sampson was fond of her. Sometimes when Phillip entered Mr. Sampson's office when he was talking to Sally, he felt that he was interrupting something.

This particular week was an important one for Phillip. It was well known that there would be an announcement on who would head up the new branch opening in the next town over. There was competition for the position from several other assistant branch managers in the region, but Mr. Sampson had assured Phillip that the combination of Phillip's skills and his longevity made him a shoo-in.

At 8:50 a.m. Phillip heard someone knocking on the front door and he made his way there to let the two tellers Maria and Stephanie in and then relocked the doors. Sally usually drove up right at nine o'clock or a few minutes later.

"Good morning," Phillip said.

"Good morning," they replied in unison.

"Did you have a good weekend?" Stephanie asked.

"Yes, I did," he said. "And you?"

"Oh, we just tried to clean up the yard from that storm. And the leaves are starting to fall, so it wasn't as easy as we thought. Dave can't bend over since he hurt his back, so I did most of the work." She laughed.

"You're a very hard worker," Phillip said. "Just be careful of your own back too."

"Oh, I will," she said.

At five minutes past nine, Sally arrived. She went to her small desk, hung up her coat in the coat room, got a cup of coffee, and said hello to everyone.

"How was your weekend, Phil?"

"Just fine, and yours?"

"Jimmy had a sleepover at our place. Four seventh-graders playing video games and eating junk food until 2 a.m. Not my idea of a relaxing weekend."

"Oh, that sounds interesting," Phillip laughed.

At ten minutes past ten o'clock, Mr. Sampson arrived, greeting everyone with his booming voice.

"Phil, you old dog, how was your weekend?"

"It was fine. I still have the boat in the water and had to check on it."

"Still in the water? Do you even use the darn thing anymore? I thought you weren't into fishing."

"I'm calling the marina today to get it hauled," he said. Phillip had forgotten about calling the marina and was glad that Mr. Sampson brought up the subject.

But the subject of the boat also sent a ripple of anxiety through Phillip's body. He immediately thought of Sofia and reached for his phone. He was about to dial but then thought better of it.

I'll run over there at lunch. That'll be easier.

The day was a normal one at the bank. They had the usual flow of elderly customers in the mornings who seemed to come simply for the social interaction.

"How are you, Mrs. Wilson?" Phillip said to the 89-year-old widow.

"Fine, Phillip." She was bent over with age and nearly faced the floor. It made it difficult to hear her.

"Did you want to see me?" he asked.

"Yes, I did." Phillip knew what she wanted to talk about but pretended it was a new subject.

"It's about that interest rate," she said. "There ain't any."

"There isn't any of what, Mrs. Wilson?"

"Ain't any interest. Your bank doesn't give interest on my money."

"Of course we pay you interest, Mrs. Wilson. It's just not much these days, with the Federal Reserve keeping interest rates very low."

"You always say that, Phillip."

"Indeed, I do, Mrs. Wilson. I'm sorry to report that interest rates are still low. But we've talked to you before about a certificate of deposit. Do you remember those discussions?"

"That's too fancy for me, Phillip."

"They're a good way to generate more interest income. Savings accounts don't produce much these days in interest."

"Too fancy."

"Well, you should consider it. Can I answer any other questions for you today Mrs. Wilson?"

"Nope."

"Well, you have a nice day. It's always a pleasure to see you."

"You're a nice young man, Phillip."

"Why thank you for saying that."

"Why can't my son act nice every now and then?"

"I don't know," Phillip said. "You might be too hard on him."

"He's meaner than a junkyard dog."

"You take care now, Mrs. Wilson."

"I will."

Phillip retired to his small office and had just sat down when his cell phone rang.

"Well, well, well," Felicia said. "Aren't you the sneaky one, Mr. Casanova."

He felt faint.

"Did you go by the house today?" he said quickly and with great severity.

"I told you I was going to leave that book."

"Oh, that's right."

"But that woman! My god, Phil. She's a character. Where did you find her?"

"I can explain everything later. But was she outside?"

"No, I let myself in and she was sitting on the couch eating celery and watching cartoons."

He took a deep breath. "Was she wearing clothes?"

"Yes, of course, she was. Why?"

"Nothing. Did she say anything to you?"

"We had a lovely conversation. She's quite engaging. I love her eyes. And she's gorgeous. Where is she from? She has an odd accent."

"Look, I can't talk right now."

"She said she couldn't go outside, which I thought was a little strange."

"Oh. I asked to her stay inside."

"And she said she couldn't have sugar."

"Mmm. I can explain later. I have to go."

31

Phillip normally had lunch at his desk, but today he was in a rush to check on his house guest. He sped to his house, left the car in the driveway, and unlocked the front door.

The TV set was on and the kitchen table was again covered in various food items from the refrigerator and the cabinets.

But Sofia was not in sight. He looked down the hallway and yelled "Sofia."

Nothing.

He raced down the hallway and looked into her bedroom. The bed was empty.

He poked his head into the bathroom. It was empty.

Walking back down the hallway he stopped in his tracks and peered into his room.

Sofia lay on top of his bed, fully clothed, facing away from the door. A half-eaten carrot sat next to her back.

He walked around the bed and sat next to her. Sofia made an odd snoring sound, her mouth partly open.

Phillip noticed the clock radio. He needed to return to work or there would be gossip since he was known for his reliability and punctuality.

He made the decision not to rouse her since a sleeping Sofia was less troublesome than a woken Sofia. He stood slowly and returned to the kitchen. Phillip hastily put some things away, then left the house and sped back to work.

The rest of the work day was uneventful, though he did find the time to mention the expected announcement of the new branch manager to Mr. Sampson.

"Oh yes, that. Well, as you know Phil, those decisions are made at the main office. But I've let my thoughts be known, rest assured."

"That's great, Mr. Sampson. I want to thank you for your support."

"I'm glad to help in any way, Phil."

"Thank you, sir."

At 5 o'clock Phillip escorted the staff to the door and let them out, then he returned to set the alarm and lock up. Mr. Sampson had left at his normal time of four-thirty.

When he pulled up in front of his house, he was stunned to see Felicia's BMW in the driveway.

32

He opened the front door to peals of laughter.

Sofia and Felicia sat on the couch ensconced in a spirited conversation.

"Oh, hi Phil," Felicia said. "I thought you'd be home by now, so I stopped by again."

He knew that was a fib.

"I see you've met Sofia," he said, hanging up his car keys on a hook.

"We're having a grand time, why don't you join us?" Felicia said.

He walked over to them and tried to gauge Sofia's mood.

"Hello, *Fillleeeep*," she said smiling.

"How was your day?" he asked, sitting down.

"It was a good day. I ate many things. But I didn't have sugar."

"That's good," he said.

"I think you put sugar some place that I cannot find."

"That is correct," he said.

Felicia watched the exchange with amusement.

"Aren't you two funny," she said.

"Sofia is fond of sugar," Phillip said.

"I like sugar," Sofia said.

"So, let her have some sugar," Felicia laughed.

"If you saw how she eats it, you might think differently," he said.

Felicia laughed. "How does she eat it?"

"With her hands."

"Her hands?"

"I like sugar," Sofia said to Felicia.

"And salt," Phillip said. "We might as well get that out there as well."

Felicia looked at Phillip and Sofia in turn, trying to ascertain the nature of their relationship.

"I like salt," Sofia said.

"There's nothing wrong with a little salt," Felicia said.

"'A little' are the key words," he said, standing. "Thanks for visiting today, Felicia."

"Oh, sit down," she said laughing. "I've only been her for twenty minutes or so. Relax."

"I'm tired," he said. "Been a long day."

"Sit," she said.

He sat.

"So how did you two meet?" Felicia asked.

"He left me out too long," Sofia said with a dramatic frown.

"Now wait," he said. "That was not my fault, and you

know that. Please."

"Left you out for too long?" Felicia said to Sofia. "Heavens, Phil, what did you do to the poor woman?"

"It's a long story," he said.

"I've got time," she said.

"You wouldn't understand," he said standing again.

"Try me," she said.

"Pretty," Sofia said sitting forward and staring at Felicia's gold-colored earrings. "May I touch?"

"Of course," Felicia said.

"Oooh," Sofia said, her eyes large with excitement. "I *like* them."

"Thank you," Felicia said.

"You are a beautiful woman," Sofia said. "I like your ear things. I don't have those things."

"Felicia, you really should get going," Phillip said, still standing.

"*Fillleeeep*," Sophia pleaded, gently fingering one of the earrings, "can I have some of these?"

"No. I don't think you need earrings," he said. "Felicia, do you mind? Please?"

33

After Felicia left, Phillip changed into some work clothes.

"I need to clean up the yard," he said to Sofia. "You stay here and watch TV. I'll be just outside."

"You do work?"

"Yes. Work in the yard. Picking up branches and rake some leaves."

"I like work."

"It would be better to stay inside," he said walking to the kitchen door.

"I like to work. I don't like that thing," she said pointing to the TV.

"I thought you liked cartoons."

"Not all the time. It makes me feel funny if I watch too long. I don't think the picture machine thing is good."

He looked at her and squeezed out a wry smile.

"I have to agree with you there. You want to work in the

yard?"

"Yes. Work, work, work. You're the boss."

"Do you promise to stay in the yard?"

"Yes. What is a yard?"

"Do you promise to stay close to me?"

"Yes, *Fillleeeep*," she said, putting hands on her hips with a smirk.

She followed him into the garage, where he gathered two rakes and a large plastic barrel.

The October weather was cool, and the sun was low, so he had to hurry.

He showed her how to rake and they collected numerous piles of debris from the storm. Phillip was self-conscious about keeping his yard clean since his neighbors were fastidious with their landscaping.

"Hey there," came a voice from the next yard.

Phillip had expected his retired neighbor, Mr. Cornish, to make an appearance.

"Hi Steve," Phillip said, keeping his eyes on the ground to discourage conversation.

"Hello," Sofia said, waving her hand and smiling.

Please don't talk to him.

"I'm Steve," he said to Sofia. "What's your name?"

"I am Sofia."

"Are you a friend of Phil's?"

"He is the boss. He kept me out too long." She smiled and commenced to rake again.

"He did, huh?"

"Yes," she said as Phil quickly walked over.

"She's renting a room briefly from me, Steve."

"Oh," he said. "That's nice."

"It's getting late, and we only have a few more minutes of daylight," Phillip said. "We're trying to hurry."

"Work, work, work," Sophia said, scraping the ground furiously with her rake.

"All right then. I'll leave you to your work. Nice to meet you, Sofia."

"Bye Steve," she said waving.

He waved back.

34

Phillip ordered pizza again. It was clear now that Sofia did not appreciate the culinary value of dead animals. He had tried to introduce her to sliced turkey and Swiss cheese sandwiches, but she nearly threw up.

He was not surprised when she furiously disassembled her sandwich, throwing the turkey on the floor.

"Bad," she told him, pointing to the flattened slices.

So plain cheese pizza was a good, though boring choice. They ate in silence.

"I like pizza," she said with her mouth full of food.

"Yes, I can tell."

"Do you like pizza?"

"Yes, I do. Perhaps not every night."

They fell silent again.

Phillip had survived three days with the emotional toll of Sofia's presence. Of course, none of it made any sense.

She could be a dream, or a hallucination, or the manifestation of a nervous breakdown. Perhaps the divorce and abandonment had hurt more than he knew.

But over the three days, he slowly incorporated the woman into his small, controlled life. It was certainly preferable to a nervous breakdown.

"Can I ask you some questions?" he said, looking into her piercing eyes. "I'm not sure I'll believe anything you say, but I think I have to ask."

"You're the boss," she said, devouring another slice of pizza.

"So, um, let me see if I get this. I appear to have left you out of the water too long."

"Yes! Why did you do that *Fillleeeep?*"

"Hang on. So, because I left you out too long, you grew, um, legs. And became a person. An odd person, but still a person."

She shrugged.

"So, I gather you've been left out of the water too long before, yes?"

"Yes. Always it's work, work, work."

"And whoever finds you is the boss?"

She nodded.

"And you have to do what they say because they're the boss."

"You're the boss."

"I got that. But in the past, how many times has this happened to you?"

She looked confused. "Pizza?" she said holding up a half-eaten slice.

"No. How many times have you had a boss? Like me?"

She shrugged. "Many."

"When was the last time this happened? You know, before me?"

"*Fillleeeep*, you ask many questions. I don't know things. A storm comes. I get stuck. A man finds me. He's the boss. Work, work, work."

"Is it always men who find you?"

"Yes. They smell funny. Catch fish. Clean fish. Salt fish. Fix net."

"No women find you?"

"Sometimes. They are mean, the women. Don't like me."

"Why don't they like you?"

Sofia laughed. "The men like me much. I like men. But they smell bad. They always want the in-out thing. Always, always."

"Mmm. The last time you were left out too long, were there cars like I have?"

She shook her head and grimaced.

"Did the boats have motors? You know, that makes a loud noise."

"I hear the sound in the water. Now boats make a noise. Not before."

"How old are you?"

"Huh?"

"When were you born?"

"Huh?" she said, reaching for a piece of pizza on Phillip's plate.

"Do you remember your mother or father?"

"You're funny," she said stuffing the entire slice into her mouth.

He sat back in his chair and crossed his arms on his chest.

"Well, that's pretty much what I expected."

35

Phillip closed his bedroom door leaving Sofia in front of the TV set. It was already past his normal bedtime of nine-fifty p.m.

His cell phone rang.

"Hello, Felicia."

"Hey, there younger brother. This is a big week for you. I forgot to mention that earlier when I was over there."

"Yes. I'm trying not to think of it. A branch manager would be a big jump for me."

"I can't believe they wouldn't give it to you. Mr. Sampson pretty much said so, right?"

"That's what he said."

"Well, Ernie and I are excited for you. After all that you've been through recently."

"I'm fine. Really."

"And now you have an interesting house guest."

"Ah, I thought you might get around to Sofia."

"Where did you meet her again?"

"It's a long story. Actually, you're part of the story."

"I am?"

"Yeah. I told the gang at the pub that you knew Sofia was looking for a place to stay and you asked me if I'd rent her a room for a while. Sorry I didn't mention that earlier."

"God, Phil. You should tell me when you do things like that."

"I'm sorry. The whole thing is kind of strange."

"So where did you meet?"

"Can we save this conversation for another day? I need to get to bed."

"Are you sleeping with her?"

"No! And why would you ask that anyway?"

"I'm just trying to figure out your relationship."

"You wouldn't consider putting her up for a while, would you?"

"You want to get rid of her?" Felicia said.

"Something like that. I like my ordered life and she's kind of messed that up a bit. But she's nice. And a little naïve."

"She's quite beautiful, Phil."

"So I gather."

"You haven't noticed! Come on, Phil. She's stunning. Her eyes are amazing. And the rest of her too. Since when were you ordained into the priesthood?"

"I'm trying to protect the poor woman, for god's sake. I'm afraid to let her meet people and go outside. She says the strangest things."

"Well, I have an idea."

"Mmm. What would that be?"

"I need someone to work in the shop. I told you Nancy quit two weeks ago."

"I forgot."

"Sofia would be perfect."

"That's not a good idea," Phillip said glancing at the clock radio.

"Why don't you let me figure that out. Something tells me she could sell a lot of jewelry."

He thought about the offer for a few seconds.

"Well, it might make it easier for me knowing she's not alone. An interesting idea."

"I could pick her up tomorrow morning and try it out."

"Huh. OK. I'm sure she'll go along with it. But you have to promise me you'll pay close attention to her. She's, you know, different."

"Does she have nicer clothes?"

"Oh, that. She's wearing Martha's left-behind clothes."

"Didn't she bring any clothes with her?"

"She came with nothing, unfortunately."

"Does she have any nice slacks or fashionable jeans? A nice blouse?"

"She came literally with nothing."

There was silence on the phone.

"Nothing except what she was wearing?" Felicia said.

"Something like that. If you need her to work in your highfalutin' gift shop, she'll need to get some clothes. I can give you a credit card and you could purchase a few things for her."

"I could do that. What does she need?"

"Everything. She needs undergarments, underwear. Things like that."

More silence.

"Well, she's wearing some now," Felicia said.

"Actually, she's wearing my underwear."

"I beg your pardon?"

"She didn't have any underwear, so I lent her some of mine. I opened a new packet of jockeys."

"I see," Felicia said slowly.

"And I suppose she needs a bra. I don't know anything about bras."

Silence.

"So, she came with nothing?" Felicia said.

"I already told you that. She's wearing Martha's clothes."

"And your underwear."

"Well, yes. I know it sounds weird, but, well, that's just the way it is. I'll tell her tomorrow morning that you'll take her shopping and then she'll work in your shop. She'll like that. Oh, one other thing. Make sure she keeps her clothes on. She takes them off now and then."

Silence.

"Thanks for the heads up, Phil. I'll keep an eye on her."

36

Phillip was taking a shower the next morning when he heard the door handle turn. He had locked it, guessing that Sofia would fail to adhere to the house privacy rules.

"*Fillleeeep!*" she yelled, pounding on the door. "I need to empty my body."

"Hang on," he yelled back, shutting off the shower. "He grabbed his towel and hurriedly dried off, wrapped it around his waist, and unlocked the door.

She stared at him without moving, looking at his body up and down.

"You have fur on your chest too," she said, reaching out and rubbing her open palm across his chest.

"Hey, stop that," he said.

"You're bloody funny," she said, stepping into the bathroom.

"What did you say?" he said.

"Huh?"

"You said 'bloody funny.'"

She shrugged and went to the toilet and started to pull down her pants. He stepped outside holding the towel tightly around his waist.

"You said 'bloody funny.' That's British slang. Have you been to Britain before?"

"I don't know, *Fillleeeep*. You ask many questions. I need to empty my body."

He closed the bathroom door and got ready for work.

They ate cereal again for breakfast and had coffee. Phillip had transferred two teaspoons of sugar to a small glass bowl and left it on the table. He got up for coffee and returned with two mugs. The sugar bowl was empty.

"Sofia, why do you keep eating all the sugar? It's bad for your teeth. And I think it makes you hyper."

She shrugged.

"Listen. Today my sister Felicia is going to come here and pick you up. She's going to take you shopping for clothes. And then you're going to go to her store and work a little with her. Is that OK?"

"I like her. She has pretty ear things. Can I have some of them?"

"Maybe later."

Phillip put a credit card on the kitchen table, said goodbye to Sofia, and went to work, arriving at his normal time and doing his normal tasks. He felt like his life was slowly, inexorably returning to something like normal. Sort of.

Later in the morning, he found time to stop into Mr. Sampson's office.

"I suppose the announcement on the new branch manager is coming," he said.

"That's what we hear, Phil. I'm sure you're a little anxious about it."

"Maybe a little. I've been hoping for something like this for a long time."

"Well, I'm keeping my fingers crossed for you, Phil."

"Thanks, Mr. Sampson."

"I assume you're coming to our Halloween staff party tomorrow after work. I know it's not your cup of tea, but you're always a good sport to dress up like a pirate. That's quite a costume."

"Sure, I'll be there. I might bring a guest."

"That would be great."

Phil expected a call from Felicia to let him know how Sofia was doing.

The call never came.

He locked up the bank at closing time and drove home, thinking about what it would be like to be a branch manager. Phillip was cautious about displaying too much interest in the position, but he was nervous. Mr. Sampson was well thought of by senior executives of the bank and his support for Phillip would clinch the deal.

37

He pulled the car into the garage. He expected to see Sofia inside but remembered that Felicia's giftshop closed at the same time as the bank, so she was probably going to drop her off at any minute.

Phillip changed into a pair of old jeans and a faded Boston Celtics sweatshirt. The thought of pizza again for dinner made his stomach swirl, so he stood in front of the open refrigerator thinking of new food ideas.

He heard Felicia's car pull into the driveway and two doors closed. The front door opened, and Sofia came in first, beaming with a radiant smile he had not seen before.

"*Fillleeeep*, do you like?" she said, raising her arms to show off her new stylish dark slacks, red silk shirt, and black shoes that exposed her toes through an opening on top.

It took Phillip a moment to notice that Sofia was wearing makeup and her hair had been altered somehow.

"Well, what do you think Phil?" Felicia said, holding two bags of items with the logo of the town's most expensive clothing store. "Isn't she gorgeous?"

"Um, yes she is," he said slowly.

Sofia stood in front of Phillip and turned her head from the left to the right, and back again.

Long, gold-colored earrings swung wildly.

"Ear things!" Sofia said.

"You look very pretty," Phillip said. He felt a strange sensation swirling in his chest and throat. He swallowed.

"Phil, you won't believe what this young woman did at the store today," Felicia said.

"Oh god, what did she do?"

"She sold more than two thousand dollars' worth of jewelry is what she did! I don't sell that much in a week, and only in the summer. She's incredible!"

"Work, work, work," Sofia said.

"Listen, I have to run now, but you and Sofia are coming over for dinner tonight. And don't you dare refuse."

"We can't do that," he said quickly.

"Be there at seven," Felicia said putting down the two bags. "Don't give me any crap, just be there and bring your stunning friend with you."

"Really? Tonight?" Phillip said.

Felicia said, "Seven," as she closed the front door.

38

Sofia carried the two bags to the kitchen table and pulled out a variety of clothing items. Phillip quickly grabbed the receipt and scanned it.

"Jeeze," he said. "Thanks, Felicia. Next time you pay."

"Oh," Sofia said reaching into her back pocket and pulling out his credit card, "here is the money thing. Can I have one?"

"No."

Sofia pulled out several colorful shirts, a pair of form-fitting denim pants, and assorted undergarments. At the bottom of one bag, she pulled out the pair of white jockey shorts that she had been wearing.

"I like this better than the other ones," she said holding the jockeys. "Stronger." She held up a new pair of pink women's underwear.

"Feel," she said, frowning. "Not strong."

"No, I get it. But that's what women wear."

She shrugged.

"Oh," she said suddenly remembering something. "Look at this." She held up a black bra. "It's to hold these," she said grabbing her left breast with her left hand. "Why do they have to hold them?"

"I don't know."

She put the bra down on the table.

"Look," she said unbuttoning her shirt and exposing her new bra. "Felicia said if they hold them up, the men will like them. Do you like them?"

"You really shouldn't show people your bra like that," he said.

"Do you like them?" she repeated. "Felicia said you would like them if they were held up."

"She said that?"

"Yes."

"OK, I like them. You can close up your shirt now."

"*Fillleeeep*, can I tell you something?"

"Sure."

"I don't like the way it feels," she said cupping her breasts in her hands from underneath. "Why do they have to be held up?"

"I really don't know."

She sighed and buttoned up her shirt.

Phillip changed back into nicer clothes and told Sofia to place the new clothes in the dresser in her room.

They pulled up to Felicia's house five minutes late. Sofia did not like driving at night and was a nervous wreck when they arrived.

"Remember," Phillip said walking to the front door. "Don't talk about bras or underwear, OK?"

"My stomach feels bad," she said. "I don't like your machine."

"No bra or underwear talk, OK?"

"Yer the boss."

Ernie answered the doorbell and welcomed them in.

"Well, well, you're the famous Sofia," Ernie said. "Come in you two."

Felicia came out from the kitchen wearing an apron.

"Hi Sofia," she said.

Sofia waved.

Ernie asked if he could get them something to drink and Phillip said they would both like some plain water.

Phillip sat on the couch while Sofia wandered the room, looking at small sculptures and vases.

"Please don't touch those things," Phillip whispered to her.

She picked up a large glass sea star ornament embedded with bands of bright colors.

"Not real," she said.

Felicia and Ernie joined them, and they sat, sipping their drinks.

Felicia regaled Ernie and Phillip with Sofia's prowess at selling jewelry.

"My god," she said, "this man came in doing what men always do in the store, peering at everything as if they are lost in space. But then Sofia went up to him as I had instructed and asked if she could help. And this guy starts explaining that he was looking for something for his wife's birthday. I joined them and before I knew it, Sofia's leading him to our most expensive case and telling him how beautiful the pieces were and how his wife would like them. She even held up some earrings to her ears to show him."

"Is that all he was looking at," Ernie chuckled.

"Ernie," she said. "Behave yourself."

"Work, work, work," Sofia said, smiling.

"So how much did he spend?" Ernie asked.

"About nine hundred bucks," Felicia said. "I was stunned."

"I like ear things," Sofia said, shaking her head to make her new earrings sway.

They chatted some more and then Felicia invited them to the dinner table.

Phillip was distracted by thoughts of the impending promotion. He calculated how far he would need to drive and what time he would need to get up each morning to reach the new branch.

The two couples sat facing each other. Sofia jumped quickly into her salad. Felicia and Ernie were amused to see her sniff the lettuce first.

"It's salad dressing," Phillip said to her. She ate quickly and with fervor. Phillip gave her more salad from the large bowl.

"She likes salad," he said.

Ernie asked Phillip about the promotion and he pretended not to be concerned by it.

Felicia pushed the main course, a pasta dish, toward Phillip and he plated some for both Sofia and himself.

"But you must be nervous," Felicia said. "I mean, you've waited so long."

"Not really," he said taking a bite of the pasta.

Phillip could be excused for being self-absorbed at this moment; so much was happening at once in his life.

But as soon as he took a bite of the pasta he froze.

It was too late.

Sofia made a guttural choking sound, and in an explosion of enormous force spit a small shrimp in her mouth across the table hitting Ernie in the chin.

There was a moment in which everyone froze, stunned and speechless.

39

"Sofia!" Phillip yelled.

Ernie stared at the errant shrimp as it lay on the table next to his plate. He picked it up with his napkin in slow motion as if it were a piece of plutonium.

Felicia stared at Sofia for a moment, her eyes wide and her mouth stretched open in amazement. Then she quickly helped clean Ernie's chin.

"She doesn't like shrimp," Phillip said. "I'm sorry I wasn't paying attention. That was my fault."

Sofia's face contorted in odd expressions as she tried to clear the taste from her mouth.

"Drink some water," Phillip said. "It'll help."

"I don't like that," Sofia said, gulping water.

"Oh, it never occurred to me to mention we were having shrimp scampi," Felicia said. "I'm sorry Sofia."

"You're sorry?" Ernie said. "How about me?"

Phillip plated more salad for Sofia, then stood and took her plate of scampi into the kitchen. Felicia followed him.

"What was that about?" she whispered.

"She doesn't like shrimp."

"Yes, but to spit it out like that?'

"Felicia, I told you several times she is different. I'm sorry she did that, but she meant no harm."

"Jeeze," she said, shaking her head. "I've never seen that before."

They both reentered the dining room.

"Now, where were we," Felica said sitting down. "Phillip, we were talking about your promotion."

"I don't have the promotion yet," he said. "I'm guessing they'll put something out on Friday."

"But you'll get it," she said. "You must be thrilled."

"I'll be thrilled after I get it."

Ernie appeared to still be in shock and slowly, self-consciously ate his scampi, keeping his head down and saying nothing.

"So, Sofia, I'll ask you since Phillip is being coy about this question: how did you two meet? I must admit to being curious about this subject now."

Phillip gave Felicia a stony look.

"He kept me out too long," Sofia said, furiously crunching through her salad.

"Out of what?" Felicia said.

"I don't know what that means," Sofia to Phillip.

"You said he kept you out too long but kept you out of *what* too long?" Felicia said. "What were you *in*?"

"Oh," Sofia said, smiling. "Water. He kept me out of the

water too long."

Felicia's and Ernie's eyes swiveled to look at Phillip.

"Hmm," Phillip said. "Can we take a pass on that question tonight?"

"No," Ernie said. "I'm dying to know. Come on, what does she mean? I had a shrimp projectile launched my way tonight and I'm curious."

Sofia ate heartily, uninterested in the conversation.

"Let's see," Phillip said slowly, "I was driving past a bus stop on the night of the nor'easter, and I saw Sofia. She was drenched waiting for the bus. So, I offered her a ride, I felt so bad for her."

"Why does she think you left her out in the rain too long?" Ernie said.

Phillip shrugged, now a firm believer in the simple declaratory value of a shoulder shrug.

Ernie and Felicia scanned the faces of Sofia and Phillip; Sofia had her head down eating her salad and Phillip stared back at them, smiling gently.

Felicia chuckled and shook her head, standing and grabbing some dishes.

"How about some desert?" she said to Phillip. "There's no shrimp in it."

"Very funny. What kind of dessert do you have?"

"Blueberry pie with ice cream. And coffee."

"She'll love that," he said. "Do you have any sugar?"

"Yes, why?"

"Don't bring any out for coffee. Just put one teaspoon in her cup."

"Ok," Felicia said slowly, making her way to the kitchen.

"I'll help," Ernie said standing and taking more plates into the kitchen.

Phillip sipped his water while Sofia finished her salad. Inside the kitchen, he could hear his sister and Ernie whispering.

40

Phillip was brushing his teeth later that evening when he suddenly stopped to stare at himself in the mirror. He had a tiny smudge of toothpaste at the right corner of his mouth.

Am I alright? Is everything OK?

He started brushing again, then stopped abruptly.

No, it's not alright. This is not normal. Sofia is not normal. Felicia looked at me in a funny way tonight.

He could hear a game show on TV from the family room. Sofia now liked game shows more than cartoons.

Phillip finished brushing his teeth and then walked to the family room. He was wearing a white tee-shirt and long pajama bottoms. Sofia was mesmerized by the show and did not acknowledge him when he sat down next to her.

"Sofia, can you look at me?"

She nodded but did not look at him.

"Sofia, look at me."

She turned.

"Tomorrow is a busy day for you. Felicia is going to come by and pick you up and take you to work."

"Work, work, work," she said.

"Tomorrow after work I'm going to take you to our company Halloween party. I think it's kind of lame, but, well, Mr. Sampson loves these bonding things."

She flashed one of those facial expressions that he learned meant she had no idea what he was talking about.

"I have to wear a costume, but I don't have one for you. Not everyone wears costumes."

She ignored him, turning back to the TV.

He stood, reached for the remote, and turned the sound down.

"Can you please change into your pajamas when you go to bed? They're on your bed. Don't take off your clothes out here."

She turned to look up at him. "I want to be in your bed tonight. I don't like it in the other place."

"That's your bedroom and I have my bedroom."

"Mmm," she uttered and turned back to the TV.

Phillip made sure the sugar was still hidden in the kitchen, then padded down the hallway, closed his door, and got into bed.

He was sleeping soundly when he woke to find Sofia had entered the bed. He turned on the light. She had buried herself under the sheets.

"Sofia, I thought I—"

But he suddenly stopped.

I'm so tired.

"Fine. Whatever. Please don't wake me, Sofia. I need to get some sleep."

He turned off the light and rolled onto his left side and away from her. He inched to the edge of the bed.

Sofia closed the distance until she was touching his back.

"Fillleeeep?"

"Yes."

"Can I touch you on the arm?"

"Fine."

She put her hand on his arm, then quickly shifted it down so that she squeezed her arm between his arm and his rib gage. She pulled closer and rested her forehead on the back of his neck, while her hand now rested on his chest.

"Go to sleep," he said. "Please."

41

The alarm clock radio came on. Phillip was gently woken from sleep with the emotional strains of the second movement of Mozart's piano concerto No. 27 playing on the local classical music station.

Phillip loved classical music but kept his interest in the subject to himself. His attempts to introduce Martha and others to the genre had been met with good-natured eye-rolling.

He yawned and stared at the digital numbers on the clock.

This was his preferred method of waking each morning; soft classical music that entered a dream and nudged him awake. Then he would stare at the numbers on the clock, fluttering his eyelids now and then, watching the inexorable changing of the numbers. After Martha had left, he stared at the numbers for longer periods, comforted in the regular and measured advance in minutes, like a steady metronome for life.

He yawned again and rolled onto his back but was startled to hear Sofia snoring in a rasping, gurgling solo that sounded musical.

Oh, I forgot.

Phillip rolled out of bed, stood, stretched, walked around the bed, and tripped over Sofia's clothes that she had tossed on the floor.

Really! What has this woman got against clothes?

He leaned down and picked up the old pair of his pajamas he had given her to wear. He noticed a pair of her new underwear had been tossed on top of the pile.

Phillip looked at her as she snored lightly. The covers and bedspread exposed half her lower extremities from the waist down. He saw her right buttocks, thigh, leg, and ankle.

He decided not to wake her, piling the pajamas on a small chair next to the bed.

Halfway through his shower, the bathroom door opened.

"Good morning, Sofia," he said.

"Hello, *Fillleeeep.* Can I get into the rain thing too?"

"No. Wait your turn."

She pulled back the shower curtain and looked at him.

"Yes please?" she said.

"No. And put some clothes on, Sofia. People don't walk around naked. Or most people, anyway."

He pulled the curtain back and finished showering. After a few minutes, he turned off the shower, pulled the curtain back, and reached for his towel. Sofia was sitting on the toilet with the seat cover down.

She frowned.

"What's wrong?" he said, toweling himself off unself-consciously as if he were in the men's locker room at the health club.

"I want to take the rain thing with you."

"It's too crowded in there. And slippery. You can take one now. Remember, you need to be ready for Felicia today. You'll need to wear some of those new clothes."

She stood and walked to the shower.

"I don't know the rain thing," she said pointing at the faucet.

Now he frowned.

"Sofia, I showed you twice how to use that."

"Mean boss," she said, turning the water on.

He left, closed the door, and got ready for work. It would be a big week in his life and excitement filtered in and out of his consciousness like a butterfly.

Later, Sofia came to the kitchen dressed in a new light-blue Rayon blouse, form-fitting denim jeans, and shoes with the open toe.

She was not wearing a bra and her breasts pressed against the thin fabric.

Sofia sat, reached for the box of cereal, filled her bowl, and poured so much milk that pieces of cereal overflowed and fell onto the table top.

"Why does it do that?" she said, grabbing the fallen pieces and tossing them into her mouth.

Phillip shrugged.

"Coffee?" he said.

"Yes. And sugar."

He had already placed two teaspoons of sugar into her mug. He put it down next to her. She used her two hands to pull the mug to her mouth. She took a sip and put it down.

"You look nice today," he said.

"You like?" she smiled.

"Yes. Felicia chose your clothes very well. They fit you nicely."

"You are a good boss," she beamed.

"But I was wondering," he said slowly, "if you wouldn't mind wearing a bra today when you work with Felicia."

"The thing that holds them up?" she said, frowning and cupping her left breast with her left hand.

"Yes, that thing. You need to wear that thing. That's what women wear. It doesn't look nice when you don't wear them."

"It hurts," she said.

"I'm sorry it doesn't feel right, but you really can't work with Felicia without a bra."

She shrugged and ripped through her cereal.

After breakfast and coffee, Phillip reminded Sofia that he was taking her to a work event later in the day. He gathered she did not know what he was talking about, nor cared particularly.

"And please, can you go put on your bra? Felicia will expect you to have a bra on. And given the shrimp episode, I don't think we should put any undue stress on my sister."

Sofia crossed her arms in front and said, "No. I don't like it."

"Please?"

"No."

He moved quickly to the only leverage he had with her. "I'm the boss."

She dropped her arms, said, "You are a mean boss," and stomped down the hall to her bedroom.

"*Fillleeeep*," she yelled after several minutes.

Oh god.

He looked at his watch and then raced down the hallway. Sofia stood in the bedroom with her blouse off holding a white bra.

"It doesn't work," she said. "The machine is wrong." She had taken to calling any object requiring manual manipulation a "machine."

He stepped in and held the bra for her to put her arms through. He had seen Martha put on a bra by herself many times and tried to show Sofia how the snaps worked by doing it behind her back.

"No good," she said.

He snapped the bra in the back and told her to tug at the straps to make the fit more comfortable. She looked at herself in the mirror.

"You like?"

"Yes, it fits nicely. Just don't forget to put on your blouse. I have to go. Have a nice day. And quit looking for the sugar, you'll never find it."

42

It was not like Phillip to feel nervous. Or if he did experience nervousness, he did not prefer to recognize it as such.

He opened the bank that morning as he normally did. The tingling in his chest and the shortened length of his inhalations he attributed to dealing with Sofia.

But it was the promotion that was on his mind. He thought of the new title, the responsibility, and even the prestige he would gain. Yes, he had been through a difficult year with the divorce and all, but the promotion would put him on solid ground. People would see him differently; he would see himself differently.

Mr. Sampson came in at his usual time and the bank hummed along busily. It was the end of the month, and activity always picked up then.

"Don't forget the costume," Mr. Sampson said to Phillip at one point. "Arrrr, matey."

"Of course not," Phillip said. "I can't wait to wear it."

Phillip hated the costume and felt foolish wearing it. Martha had bought it for him and made him wear it to the company event several years ago, at which point it had become a much talked about part of the office Halloween party legend.

But he still hated wearing it.

At lunch, Phillip decided to drive by Felicia's store out of curiosity to see how Sofia was doing.

He was also going out of caution. While he was feeling more comfortable with Sofia's presence in his life, he was mortified whenever she was out of sight. Especially with other people.

He parked in front and when he entered the little bell over the shop door tinkled brightly.

"Phil," Felicia said, sitting behind the register.

He scanned the small gift shop, and his heart took a hop.

"Where's Sofia?" he asked.

"I don't know. I thought she was with you?" Felicia said.

"Oh god," he said turning around.

"Phil!" she yelled after him.

He stopped.

"She's in the bathroom. That was a joke. You seem kind of high-strung these days!"

"Oh, aren't you the jokester," he said lamely. "Is she alright?"

"Of course, she's alright, why would you ask?"

"Come on, Felicia, you know what I mean. Is everything OK?"

"Yes, she sold another grand in jewelry this morning to two young women that wandered in. Sofia is quite chatty and engaging. She makes people feel special."

"I'm glad. Did she spit any more shrimp at people?"

"No. That was a simple mistake. Poor thing doesn't like seafood."

"Tell that to Ernie."

"Ernie is too judgmental," Felicia said.

He stared at her for a second. "I've never heard you talk that way about Ernie."

Felicia's face flushed.

Sofia appeared from the back of the store.

"*Fillleeeep!*" She rushed over and hugged him, placing her head on his chest.

Phillip felt a small swoon. Sofia had never hugged him before, and except for last night when she snuggled against him in bed, she had not touched him.

She let go of him and beamed a huge, melting smile at him.

"Felicia says you are a good worker," he said.

"I like Felicia."

"Felicia likes you," Felicia laughed.

"I need to return to work," he said. "I'll see you at home later today. Remember tonight we need to go to a work event."

Sofia shrugged.

"You're not taking her to that dreadful Halloween party the bank puts on?" Felicia said.

"Yes, I am. I just need to watch what she eats."

43

There was a titter of low-level excitement at the bank for the rest of the day, which was common for the employees in anticipation of the company party.

Phillip was his normal, steady self, even when Maria teased him a bit about his pirate costume.

"Aaarr, captain," she said in the break room.

"Maybe I won't dress up this year," he said.

"You must," she said. "It makes it easier for the rest of us to dress up."

"Are you still coming as Snow White, like last year?" he said.

"You'll just have to wait and see."

Maria's Snow-White attire was the talk of the party last year since she wore a low-cut costume accompanied by a push-up bra that had Mr. Sampson spending more time in conversation with her than was normal.

Sally, the head teller, was in the break room as well and she chuckled at the interchange. Phillip had noted a slight change in Sally's behavior recently and wondered if she was being considered for his position once the promotion was announced. It would be a good move for her.

After setting the alarm and locking up, Phillip rushed home. Felicia and Sofia were already there when he arrived. They both had coffee cups from Dunkin' Donuts in their hands while they sat on the couch.

"How is everyone?" he asked. "Big day at the store?"

"Another stellar day of commercial activity," Felicia said. "But there is one minor problem that we need to talk about."

Phillip froze as he hung up the car keys on the hook.

"What happened now?"

"Well, it seems that Sofia doesn't know what her Social Security number is, and of course I'll need that to pay her. Can you help me with that?"

"Um, that might be difficult."

"Well, how do you propose I pay her?"

"Why do you have to pay her?"

"Don't be silly, Phil. The woman is generating a lot of income for me. She needs to get paid. Right Sofia?"

Sofia was in the middle of taking a huge sip of coffee.

"Me?" she said, looking confused.

"You need to get paid, right Sofia?"

"Yes," Sofia said.

"Can't you pay her under the table?" he said.

"That's illegal Phil and you know it."

"But this once? Really, who's going to know."

"I would."

"Well, it will take a long time to get her Social Security number, that's all I'm saying."

After a few minutes, Felicia stood and walked to the kitchen with her empty coffee cup. By now Sofia could turn on the TV set herself and she jumped at the controller, quickly flashing through channels.

"Phil," Felicia said in a low voice, "is she an undocumented immigrant? Is that what the problem is? She has a strange accent."

"Yes, something like that."

"How can I pay her? She deserves to be paid for her work."

"Maybe you could give her some merchandise? She likes earrings. And maybe a necklace?"

"I hadn't thought about that," she said. "Interesting idea. Though it's still illegal."

They both turned to look at Sofia on the couch, flipping through channels like it was a deck of cards.

"She's a special person," Felicia said. "You're lucky you found her."

"I suppose. It's a complicated situation."

After Felicia left Phillip went up into the attic to find his costume. He returned to his bedroom and put the pieces on the bed.

He did hate the costume.

Martha had wanted to buy him a costume resembling the character Jack Sparrow in the film "Pirates of the Caribbean." But when he balked, they agreed on a slightly more refined version that involved tall black boots of faux leather, dark-blue pants, a long maroon, eighteen-century military-style coat with fake gold buttons. Protruding from the jacket sleeves were white, frilly laced cuffs. There was also a matching, maroon-colored tri-cornered hat with a long black-haired wig attached inside the cap. And there was a fake plastic sword that fit in a plastic scabbard attached to a wide, faux leather belt.

It took him twenty minutes to put it on, and he finally looked at himself in the mirror.

This is ridiculous.

"Sofia," he said stomping down the hallway in his unwieldy boots, "we have to leave now."

She turned on the couch to look at him and yelped, her beaming eyes the shape of huge, tarnished silver dollars.

"No!" she said.

"It's me, Sofia. Look." He removed the hat-wig combination. "It's a costume."

Her odd, startled expression was one that he had not seen before.

"Sofia, can't you see it's me? It's Phillip. Look."

She clutched the TV controller to her chest as if were a talisman to protect her.

"We have to leave now," he said, grabbing the keys off the hook.

44

Sofia refused to look at him as they drove to the country club where the event was being held.

"It's a costume," he said. "These are just clothes. It's not that big of a deal. You surprise me sometimes."

"I don't like."

"Why? It's a costume."

She shook her head and turned away.

"Promise me that you won't eat anything at this party without checking with me."

She kept her gaze out the side window into the cool night air.

"And don't remove any clothes. Or look for sugar. You got that?"

She shrugged.

"Are you unhappy about something?" he said.

She shrugged again.

"Bad boss."

"Just keep your clothes on. PLEASE."

By the time they parked and were walking up the steps of the country club, Sofia had softened a bit, though she refused to touch him or come close, walking several feet to his side.

The reception room was loud and packed with an assortment of employees, their significant others, senior executives from headquarters, and bustling waitstaff. Phillip was not fond of these social conclaves but saw it as his duty to demonstrate leadership and a comfort level—albeit entirely fake—with social gatherings.

"Remember," he whispered to Sofia, "you're my friend. We're just friends."

"Is there beer here?"

"Why not have a Diet Coke?"

"I like the beer. Makes my head feel funny."

Before they could find the drink station, they were intercepted.

"Arrr, matey!" said Mr. Sampson, holding a beer and grinning. He never wore a costume to this event.

"Oh, hello Mr. Sampson. Hello Sally."

Mr. Sampson did not look at Phillip, but only at Sofia.

"And who is *this*?" he beamed.

"This is Sofia," Phillip said. "She's a friend of mine."

Sofia smiled. "I'm friend."

"Well, welcome to our Halloween party Sofia. It's a pleasure to meet some of Phillip's friends."

Sally's eyes shot back and forth between Phillip and Sofia.

"So, how did you two meet?" Sally said, taking a side glance at Mr. Sampson who was leaning in toward Sofia.

"He kept me out too long," Sofia said, making a wouldn't-you-know-it shrug.

"Really?" Mr. Sampson said.

"Ha, she always says that," Phillip said. "She's hilarious."

"Where are you from?" Sally said. "You have an interesting accent."

Just then Maria dressed again as Snow White with her push-up bra joined the group.

There was another round of introductions and everyone stared at Sofia with enormous curiosity. Phillip was tiring of Sofia's effect on people. He was also starting to perspire under the wig.

"Hey folks, Sofia and I will just grab a drink and circle back," he said, grabbing Sofia's arm and leading her away.

"Arrr," Mr. Sampson said.

On the way to the drink stand, Phillip said hello to several people he knew but kept pushing Sofia past the throng. They stood in the small drink line, and he was thrilled to be away from Mr. Sampson.

"That was my boss," Phillip said. "I think he liked you."

"Is he a good boss or a bad boss?"

"I think he's a good boss. He's been good to me. And he recommended me for the promotion, so I think he's a good boss."

"Mmm," she said.

"Other lady funny."

"Maria? Oh, she always wears that costume. I think it's inappropriate, to be honest. But I guess there's no harm done. She's very nice."

"Other lady."

"That's Sally. She's the head teller. They might move her into my position when I get the promotion."

"Your boss and the lady. Funny."

"And what can I get for you two," the bartender said, smiling at Sofia.

"Beer," she said.

"Sure, what kind?"

"With bubbles," she said.

The bartender laughed and smiled grandly at her.

"She'd like a light beer," Phillip said. "Any light beer."

The bartender never took his eyes off Sofia.

"With bubbles," she repeated.

"Of course," he said. "And you sir," he said finally addressing Phillip.

"The same, please."

It was a cash bar and Phillip left a dollar tip in the bowl.

He led her off to the side and away from the crowd. He also made a surprising discovery.

Phillip *liked* having Sofia around him, whether it was at home or in public. She had a strange effect on people, but she also had a strange effect on *him*. Sofia was odd, of course, but she was not judgmental about Phillip as a *person*. She didn't like his choice of food, or his driving, or his hiding sugar, but she seemed to like *him*, and genuinely so. And the fact that other people found her so beguiling also made him feel good.

"So, you like my boss," he said sipping his beer.

She shrugged.

He laughed. "So, you *don't* like my boss."

"He is a man. Always the in-out thing. Always."

Phillip leaned in. "You really shouldn't talk about that here. It's not polite. I don't know much about Mr. Sampson's personal life. He has a wife and kids, but never brings his wife to company outings."

"The other lady is his wife."

"No. Sally is the head teller. Not his wife."

She shrugged. "They do the in-out thing."

Phillip's right hand was inches from his mouth with the glass of frothy beer when he froze.

"They *don't* do the in-out thing, Sofia!"

"Yes, they do. You're funny. I like the other lady. Can I have a dress like hers?"

"Wait!" he said grabbing her forearm. "Do you think Sally and Mr. Sampson are doing the in-out thing?"

She saw the alarm in his face and waited a moment to respond.

"Not here," she said carefully, taking a sip.

"Of course, not here," he said. "But elsewhere?"

"Is that bad?"

"Well, I mean—he's married, Sofia. He has a wife."

"So?"

"So, that would be a big deal. And if he's sleeping with Sally—Jeeze, that's against company policy." Phillip took a big gulp of his beer.

"You know," he said, chuckling, "you have a wild imagination, Sofia. I'll give you that much."

"Not sleeping," she said. "The in-out thing. Not sleeping."

He shook his head and laughed. "You're too much."

She took his left hand, pulled it over, and flattened it against her stomach.

"Can I eat food?" she said. "My stomach begs for food. It is a begging stomach."

"Of course, let's go find some food. I'll supervise. We don't want any more projectile shrimp."

Phillip was able to lead Sofia through the buffet line, loading her plate with salad and vegetables. At one station a woman wearing a chef's hat loomed over a red slab of prime rib. Sofia started to gag, and he quickly led her away to a table with several other employees. Sofia barely raised her head at the table while she devoured her food. Phillip did his best to socialize.

45

Later that night Phillip got ready for bed and set Sofia up in front of the TV.

"I go to bed now," she said standing.

"Um, OK. Don't forget to put on your pajamas. And please leave them on."

She shrugged and followed him down the hall to their bedrooms.

Phillip went into the bathroom and brushed his teeth.

He was joined by Sofia who had quickly changed into his old pajamas. They brushed their teeth together, never exchanging a word as if they had done this for forty years.

"Good night," he said to Sofia.

"Good night," she said, following him into his room.

He stopped, turned, and pointed toward her room.

"Please Sofia, that's your room."

But she was already under the covers. She reached her

arm out and patted his area of the bed.

"Sofia, promise me you'll keep your pajamas on."

She nodded, her eyes closed.

He crawled into bed, turned off the light, and lay on his side facing the clock radio and away from Sofia.

When she inched forward, he did not protest. She wedged her right hand between his arm and chest. Phillip was not immune to Sofia's beguiling effect, nor was he unconscious of her stunning physical beauty.

Yet like many areas of his life, Phillip had placed Sofia in a compartment that only she occupied. He could observe her and take her out of the compartment now and then but would treat her like all the other items in his personal cupboard—with cautious respect.

In fact, Phillip did feel a mild excitement, but it was about tomorrow's announcement of his promotion. He tried to calm himself by fluttering his eyelids to glimpse the slow, methodical changing numbers on the clock radio.

Unconsciously he placed his hand over Sofia's hand on his chest but immediately removed it.

She grabbed his hand and covered it with hers.

Who cares? It's a hand, that's all. Go to sleep. Big day tomorrow.

Later that night Phillip dreamed that he was in a large room, with many people he did not know, and several that he did, including Mr. Sampson. In the dream, there was a reason why people had gathered in the room, but Phillip could not understand what that reason was. Mr. Sampson spoke to Phillip in the dream. He said, "Arrr." Phillip replied, "Arrr."

At some point in the night, Phillip woke to the sound of Sofia snoring. When she snored, the sound was like that of a diesel engine just starting up—loud, rumbling that transitioned to a low throbbing purr.

He marveled at how much noise she could make when she slept. Martha, he noted, made almost no sound when she slept, as if she were paralyzed.

The clock showed 2:42 a.m. He watched it off and on until he fell asleep.

In the morning he showered as he normally did. At one point he heard her come in, put the toilette seat down, and sit. When he finished, he pulled back the curtain and grabbed his towel, drying himself off.

She was naked and her hair was a disheveled mess. Phillip was thinking of his new position as branch manager.

"I like your body," she said, yawning. "You have fur."

"I know. I came that way." He shrugged.

"You are happy?" she said standing walking over to the shower to turn it on.

"Me? Gee, I don't know. Maybe."

"Scratch back," she said, turning away from him.

He looked and saw a long red welt near her spine.

"What happened to your back?"

"Scratch."

Phillip gently scratched her back near the welt. She arched her back.

"Good."

"Remember, Felicia is coming again today. Tell her not to give you any more makeup."

"I like it. Do you like it?"

"Yes, you look very nice with makeup. But you don't need anymore."

She turned to face him.

"You are a nice boss. A good boss."

"Well, thanks Sofia. And you're a nice—" he struggled for a second— "guest."

She smiled and turned on the shower.

He went into his room and got dressed, choosing a blue button-down Oxford dress shirt with a dark-blue sweater vest.

Sofia finally joined him at the kitchen table, dressed nattily in a pair of dark-brown slacks, a white, long-sleeve shirt with a thin cashmere maroon sweater. He was thrilled to see she was wearing a bra.

"You look very nice today," he said.

"You look very nice today," she replied.

"Thank you," he said.

"Thank you," she said.

"I'm going to give you a treat today because it's my big day."

She turned her head sideways and looked at him through narrow, suspicious eyes.

"What is 'treat'?"

He stood and poured coffee into her mug and brought it over to her.

"I put two extra teaspoons of sugar in your coffee today," he said.

She clapped her hands together. "More sugar!"

He laughed.

46

Phillip nearly forgot the passcode to the alarm system and stood in front of the beeping panel in a panic. He had never done that before and closed his eyes to collect his thoughts.

Relax. Deep breath. The numbers will come to you.

And the six digits did come to him and he disarmed the system.

You need to get your act together. Is this how you're going to react to the stress of running a branch by yourself? Get a grip.

Later that morning the bank was purring along nicely, with several people waiting in line before the two tellers, one of which was Sally.

Phillip had just finished reviewing a home equity line of credit application filled out by Mr. Sacchetti, a widower who was struggling with the loss the prior year of his wife

Frannie. They were a sweet couple, and Phillip attended the small funeral service for her.

His desk phone rang.

"Phillip, could you stop in when you get a chance?" Mr. Sampson said. Even though the two offices were right next to each other, Mr. Sampson preferred to use the office phone to communicate with employees.

"Sure thing," he responded.

He walked into Mr. Sampson's office.

"Sit down, Phil. I have some information for you that I know you've been waiting for."

He sat down, crossed his legs, leaned back, and tried to act nonchalant.

"First off, I want you to know what an incredibly valuable employee you are to this branch and by extension, the entire bank. You've spent many a long hour helping us become the biggest bank in this town."

"Thank you, Mr. Sampson."

"I want to make sure you understand that, before I talk to you about the new branch they're opening nearby."

"Of course." Phillip's fingers were interlocked over his protruding right knee and he felt a minute twitch in his thumbs.

"You see, the company has a mandate for more diversity in the workplace."

"Yes, we're all very supportive of that," Phillip said.

"And, well, let me just get it out of the way—they've decided to promote Sally to lead up the new branch."

Phillip found that he had stopped breathing. His eyes were no longer focused on Mr. Sampson's eyes but were now staring at a large freckle on Mr. Sampson's cheek.

"Excuse me?" Phillip heard himself say.

"They've decided to promote Sally, Phil. They would like to have more women in positions of authority in the branches."

"But Sally has only been in banking for about two years. And she's only been a head teller for a year." Phillip licked his lips reflexively. Mysteriously they had dried and were leathery and coarse.

"I'm sorry, Phil. But there will be more opportunities at the bank. You'll see. We're expanding rapidly, as you well know."

"Excuse me, Mr. Sampson, but don't we have seven current branches?"

"Yes, that's correct."

"And aren't five of the branches managed by women?"

"Um, I don't know. I never counted."

"No, it's true. The new branch will bring the total to eight branches, and if Sally is branch manager, then that will bring the total of women-managed branches to six out of eight. That means that seventy-five percent of the branches will be managed by women."

"I suppose that's right. You were always good with math," Mr. Sampson said.

"But didn't you recommend me for the position?"

"Of course, I did."

Before Phillip could stop himself, he blurted out: "And did you recommend Sally for the position as well? You had to have recommended her."

"I might have. Let me think. Yes, I did, Phil. But I felt

she'd be good at the position."

Phillip stared at the freckle and felt many emotions roil through his brain, some of which he understood and some of which he didn't.

"I'm sorry," Mr. Sampson said. "Your time will come."

Phillip did not move but stared at the freckle with increased intensity.

"Phil? Hey Phil, are you OK?"

Phillip sighed, released his interlocked fingers over his knee, stood up, and returned to his desk.

The remainder of the day was a smudge for him since he barely understood what he was doing. Sally and he avoided each other, and she asked to leave a few minutes early, rushing out before Maria and even Mr. Sampson.

At home, Phillip pulled the car into the garage and sat with the car off, staring through the windshield at the assorted garden tools hanging from hooks in the garage. He felt tired.

47

Sofia was sitting in front of the TV watching an old western movie. Without looking up, she said, "Did you have a good day, *Fillleeeep*?"

"Yes," he said.

Why did you say that? It was a horrible day.

"We have pizza tonight, *Fillleeeep*?"

He sighed. "I suppose. Actually, let's go to the pub."

Her eyes lit up. "Let's go to pub!"

Phillip trundled into his bedroom, sat on the bed, and slowly took off his business clothes. He barely noticed Sofia come into the room.

Sally? Really? I can't believe it. I can't. Something's wrong.

He hung up his slacks and threw his shirt into a small hamper he kept in his room.

"*Fillleeeep*, why are you sad?"

He was too involved in his internal dialogue to notice her.

"*Fillleeeep.*"

"Yes?"

"You are sad."

"Perhaps just a bit."

"Why are you sad?"

"I don't know."

"A bad thing happen?"

"Yes. For me, at least. Not for Sally."

"Sally other work woman?"

"Yes."

"She like your boss."

He was in the process of slipping on a pair of jeans and stopped.

"You think Sally and my boss are doing the in-out thing?"

She nodded. "Is that bad?"

He sighed and finished pulling on his jeans.

"Sally," he said shaking his head. "I can't believe it."

He threw on a sweatshirt and a pair of old sneakers.

"Let's go to the pub and grab some dinner," he said.

They sat on two stools at the bar and ordered beers. Sofia spun around on her stool 360 degrees several times before Phillip begged her to stop.

"Bad boss," she said, taking a huge sip of beer.

"Yes, I am a bad boss. A stupid boss. A clumsy idiotic boss."

She turned to peer at the side of his face.

"You are sad."

"I suppose."

"You don't like your boss?"

"Not anymore. How can he be sleeping with her?" he said, turning to Sofia.

"What?"

"Are you completely sure that my boss and Sally are sleeping with each other?"

"Sleeping?"

"Are they doing the in-out thing?"

"Oh, I see. Yes, they are doing the in-out thing. Yes."

"How do you know?"

"Mmm," she said, thinking.

"I don't know. But I can see in their eyes."

"And you think Sally and my boss are sleeping together, and not my boss and Maria, the other lady?"

"Boss and Sally," she said, taking another sip. "My head feels funny."

"My head feels funny," he said glumly.

"*Fillleeeep*, my stomach cries for food. Please can we have food?"

"Oh Jeeze, of course. Hey Dave," he said to the bartender. "Can we see some menus?"

"Sure thing Phil."

He ordered a large Caesar salad for Sofia and mentioned twice to Dave that the kitchen must omit the anchovies. He ordered a grilled chicken sandwich for himself.

Dave kept hanging around, trying to start a conversation with Sofia, but she was intent on devouring her salad. Phillip only ate half his sandwich and nibbled at a few French fries.

Sofia finished her salad and finished his French fries.

"I like," she said.

"Be my guest," he smiled wanly.

Phillip also did something he had not done in many years. He drank three beers over the length of the evening at the pub. Sofia drank two beers but did not finish her third one.

Toward the end of the evening, Dave asked Phil how he and Sofia had met.

"I left her out too long," he said. "It was my fault."

"His fault," Sofia said.

"Interesting," Dave said.

Phillip paid and they left, with Sofia clinging to his arm.

"I am upside down," she said, walking to the car.

"Me too," he said. He drove slowly home and pulled into the garage.

Sofia burped loudly when they entered the kitchen.

He laughed.

I think I'm a little tipsy. That was stupid. You'll be hurting tomorrow at work.

Phillip sat down at the kitchen table and Sofia laid out on the couch.

"Sofia, I think Felicia is going to pick you up again tomorrow for work. And I have to work as well."

"Work, work, work," she said, her eyes closed.

"I have to go to bed now and so should you," he said standing.

"I am upside down," she said.

He walked to the couch and stood over her.

"Sofia, you really shouldn't sleep out here."

She opened her eyes and looked up.

"You are sad."

"OK. I'm sad."

"Now I am sad."

"You don't have to be sad, Sofia. One sad person in this house is enough. Come." He reached out with his hand and she grabbed it, pulling herself to a seating position.

She grabbed his hand and pulled herself up. He held her hand and led her back to her bedroom.

"Goodnight Sofia. I'll wake you in the morning."

She flopped onto her bed face down, arms sprawled.

He looked down at her, realizing she was still clothed.

I'm not going to put her pajamas on. She can sleep like that.

Phillip undressed, put on a pair of pajama bottoms and an old tee shirt. He brushed his teeth and stared at himself in the mirror.

Yes, I am sad. So what? People don't always get what they want.

He got into bed, turned on his side facing the clock radio, and turned off the lights.

He heard Sofia come into the room.

"*Fillleeeep,*" she said, getting under the sheets. "I'm upside down in my head."

48

Many things had changed in Phillip's life that day. The orderly unfolding of normal routine at the bank had been broken, perhaps forever. He was not going to get the new branch manager's position. The bank employees would look at him differently. Mr. Sampson would make more promises about the future that he might not keep. Martha might even gloat when she found out. He was indeed sad.

And angry.

If Sofia was correct, Mr. Sampson and Sally were sleeping together.

He did not like feeling angry, an emotion he resisted with every fiber in his body. Still, to think he had been lied to by Mr. Sampson upset him.

Phillip lay in bed staring at the numbers on his clock radio. At least those numbers were orderly and followed the rules. They did the same thing over and over again. They never disappointed. They never mocked.

Sofia scrunched over toward him in the bed. She squeezed her hand between his arm and chest and snuggled more tightly against his back. He felt her breasts against his back and her thighs against his.

For god's sake, Sofia you're naked. Why do you do that?

He turned onto his back to look at her in the dark.

"You need to put your pajamas on," he said. "Then come back to bed if you like."

She pressed her head against his shoulder and rubbed her hand against the hairs on his chest.

"I like your fur," she said.

"Pajamas," he said. Sofia's face was barely visible from the glow of the clock radio LED numbers.

She leaned on her elbow and raised up so that her face was inches from his.

"Sofia, please," he said. "Pajam—."

She kissed him quickly before he finished saying "pajamas."

He lay still. She kissed him again, this time slowly and with great tenderness.

"Please stop," he said.

She did not stop, and he suddenly felt like he had fallen through a trapdoor of profound passion. He could not control himself. Phillip was soon naked, and Sofia completely and utterly enveloped him in her sensuality and lovemaking.

Phillip was not an experienced lover and had few experiences with women besides Martha. He discovered something breathtakingly new with Sofia—lovemaking with her was fifty percent *give* and fifty percent *take*. With Martha, it seemed like lovemaking was one hundred percent *give* on his part. It was not reciprocal; it had been uniformly one-sided.

He did not know how long their lovemaking lasted and he did not care. He finally fell asleep exhausted, sweating, and calm.

The alarm went off and he found himself staring at the clock radio numbers. He yawned and suddenly realized what had happened the previous night. Phillip turned in bed and saw that Sofia was not there. He wondered briefly whether he had imagined their previous night's lovemaking.

Phillip stood and walked naked throughout the house looking for Sofia. He looked in the bathroom and the guest bedroom, but she was not there.

He walked into the kitchen and family room. She had disappeared. Phillip retraced his steps and searched the house again.

"Sofia," he called out. "Where are you?"

After fifteen minutes of this, Phillip felt a strange rush of *déjà vu*. It was the same disorienting, panicky feeling he experienced when he first discovered Sofia resting underwater at his mooring.

He went into the garage and checked to see if she was in the car, but she was not there. He went back into the kitchen and looked through the blinds onto the front yard. The sun had just risen smearing the sky with a pinkish glow to the east.

Sofia sat in the front yard with her pajamas on and a

blanket around her shoulders. She was staring over the tops of the trees at the sunrise.

He threw on a long raincoat over his naked body and walked out to her.

"Sofia," he said. "Please come inside. It's cold out here."

She turned to look at him.

Phillip was stunned to see she had been crying. Sofia had not learned to take off her makeup at night and the remaining mascara was blotchy, ringing her eyes in black.

"I lie," she said, sniffling. "I lie to you."

49

Inside the house, Phillip made coffee and tried to calm Sofia, but she was upset and avoided eye contact. He took off his long raincoat and hung it up. Phillip was naked again but was unconcerned. It seemed natural to him now.

She sat at the kitchen table with the blanket around her shoulder. Pieces of grass and several twigs stuck to the fleece blanket.

"Do you not want to go to work with Felicia today?" he asked.

"No. Not work."

"OK. I'll text her." He picked up his phone and texted his sister that Sofia was not feeling well and would not be going to work.

"Do you want to tell me what's wrong?" he said, bringing over two cups of coffee. "I gave you extra sugar."

She exchanged a pained smile but said nothing.

"Maybe I'll call in sick today," he said. "Believe it or not, I've never called in sick before. Maybe today I'll be sick. I do feel kinda sick." Phillip was talking to himself.

He picked up his phone, dialed a number, listened, and then pushed several numbers while listening to prompts. Finally, he said, "Mr. Sampson, this is Phillip. I'm afraid I'm not feeling well today and won't be in. I have no appointments, so no customers need to be contacted for rescheduling. Thank you."

"That wasn't so hard," he said, again speaking to himself.

He suddenly felt inexplicably giddy.

"Let's do something today," he said. "Let's go for a ride. There's a famous art gallery about an hour away that I haven't been to in years. Let's go."

Sofia drank her coffee and finally looked up at him with her raccoon-like eyes.

"What's wrong, Sofia?"

"I make a lie."

"What did you lie about?"

She shrugged. "It makes me sad."

"Well, you're making me sad. So, tell me, what did you lie about?"

She stood up, dropped the blanket from around her shoulders, and turned her back to him. She lifted the baggy pajama top to expose her back.

"Sofia, what happened to your back!" Phillip rushed over and held the pajama top up and looked at the huge, vertical welts on her back. Several had started to bubble up as if she had suffered a burn.

She pulled the pajama top away from Phillip's hand and

turned to face him.

"I have to go to the water," she said.

"What do you mean? I don't understand. Please sit down, you don't look well."

She sat and pulled the blanket around her shoulders again.

"I have to go back," she said, twisting her mouth in a nervous gesture and looking down at her coffee mug.

"Go back where?"

"To the water."

"Why? Are you sick?"

"Yes."

"What kind of sickness do you have?"

She sighed. "If I don't go back soon, I get very sick."

Phillip had made a conscious decision to accept Sofia's presence in his life because he could not explain in a logical, rational way why she existed. At one point he thought perhaps he had imagined she existed.

Yet, Sofia worked at his sister's store, was introduced to his former wife, and even met his boss. While he took succor in the knowledge that other people confirmed her existence, in the back of his mind he sometimes wondered about his own perceptions. Now, after an unusual day and unusual night, sitting naked at his kitchen table he could only think of his powerful yearning for Sofia.

"Sofia, why did you say you lied to me?"

She sighed again, her whole body rising up and down like a gentle ocean swell.

"You did not keep me out too long," she said taking a timid sip of coffee.

"At the boat you mean?"

She nodded.

"You were a different shape when I brought you aboard, and then you changed and had legs. Is that what you're talking about?"

She nodded.

"You said I left you out of the water for too long."

"Yes."

"That was a lie?"

"Yes."

"Then what really happened at the boat?"

"I pretend to be dead. When you go into boat I change." She patted her thighs.

"So, you changed because you wanted to, not because I left you out too long?"

"Yes."

"You said other things to me, like whoever finds you is your boss."

She shrugged.

"Was that a lie?"

"Little lie," she said, holding up her hand showing a small distance between her thumb and forefinger.

"Why are you telling me that now? What's wrong with your back?"

She exploded in tears, squeezing her black-ringed eyes tight as the salty water streamed down her cheeks.

Phillip stood and walked over to her and knelt.

"Hey Sofia, relax. Everything will be OK."

"Not OK," she cried. "Not OK. Don't want to go to the water."

"Then don't go. Stay with me."

This made Sofia cry with more fervor. She stood and rushed back to her bedroom, slamming the door shut.

50

Phillip sat naked at the kitchen table for several minutes, drinking his coffee and thinking. After a while, he felt chilly and went into his bedroom to put on some clothes. Afterward, he knocked on Sofia's door.

"Can I come in?"

She didn't answer, so he opened the door.

Sofia was under the covers crying quietly. He sat on the edge of the bed.

"Sofia, come on. Speak to me."

"No. I go to the water now. Now."

He pulled back the covers, but she yanked the covers back over her.

Phillip left the covers in place and tried to coax her out.

"Do you need to go like *right* now?"

"Yes."

"What will you do when you go to the water?"

She pulled back the covers and looked through her black-ringed eyes.

"Don't understand," she said.

"If I take you down to the water now, what do you need to do? Get into the water like when I first saw you?"

She nodded.

"Then will you be OK? How long do you need to be in the water before you can come out again? I mean with legs?"

She peered closely at his face as if looking for something she could not find.

"I cannot get out of water for a long time. Or I get sick. Very sick."

"Um, OK. When will you be back?"

"Back?"

"Yes, when can I see you again?"

She started crying.

"Sofia, I want to see you again. Are you saying that you're not coming back? Ever?"

"Long time," she said, sniffling and wiping her nose with the back of her wrist.

"How long? Days, months, years?"

"Many," she said. "Many, many."

Phillip looked down on Sofia. He reached out with his hand and gently stroked her forehead, then brushed the hair away from her face.

"You look silly," he said quietly, trying to smudge some of the mascara away with his thumb. He was already thinking about other things.

She's so beautiful. And childlike. And a kind lover.

"Sofia, why did you let me take you out of the water at

the boat? I mean, if you knew you were going to trick me into believing I was your boss—" he chuckled at the image— "what was the point? You knew you would have to go back. You've only been out of the water for about a week. Why did you bother doing this?"

Sofia sniffled, lifted her hand from under the covers, and wrapped her free arm around his thighs.

"I miss you," she said snuggling her head against his hip. "I have a pain inside when I don't see you."

He ran his fingers gently through her hair.

"We've never met before, Sofia. Believe me, I'd remember you."

He could feel her head shaking back and forth against his hip. "No. Many times we meet. I always remember. You always forget. Always same."

Phillip's fingers froze against her scalp.

"We've met before?"

"Yes."

"How many times?"

"Many."

"Like how many?"

"Many, many."

"I have a hard time believing that, Sofia. I'd remember you."

"Always forget. This time you are more kind. You give me sugar. And you have a bad boss this time."

He sighed. "Yes, I have a bad boss."

"You leave bad boss and go to new boss."

"Where would I go, to one of the big national banks? I'd be lost there."

"*Fillleeeep*, you must go to new boss."

"You think so?" he said, starting to stroke her hair again.

She nodded.

They sat in silence while he stroked her hair and she snuggled against his hip.

"You have to go?" he said.

51

The car pulled up in front of Felicia's store and Phillip honked. Out came his sister and bent down to the passenger side window that was open.

"Sofia, I can't believe you're leaving us," she said reaching in and putting her arm around Sofia.

"I go home," she said. "Am sick."

"Oh you poor thing," Felicia said. "You've been such a bright light in my life these past few days! Will you come back when you feel better?"

"Yes."

"You promise to come to visit me in the store?"

"Yes. Promise."

Felicia leaned in and kissed Sofia on the cheek. "Safe travels. We'll miss you, Sofia."

Sofia started crying, and Felicia glanced at Phillip, but he refused to look at her.

"We need to go," he said. "I'll call you later."

They drove back to his house and he made more coffee. He pulled out the hidden sugar bowl and put it in the middle of the kitchen table.

"Have as much as you want," he said, but she avoided looking at it until he turned away. At which point she grabbed a handful and stuffed it clumsily into her mouth. The crystals fell onto her chin and spread out across the tabletop.

He returned with two mugs and used his hand to scrape away some of the sugar to put his mug down.

"So, Sofia, if we've met many times before—"

"Many, many" she interrupted.

"OK, so, was I always like this?"

"What?"

"Did I drive a car? Work in a bank?"

"No."

"What did I do the last time we met?"

"Catch fish," said, grimacing.

"Was I nice to you?"

"No."

"Then it wasn't me. I'm nice. I don't catch fish."

She smirked. "*Fillleeeep*, you are the same *Fillleeeep*. Always same."

"OK, what did I do before I was a fisherman? You said we've met many times. So, before I was a fisherman, what did I do?"

She closed her eyes, which Phillip had never seen her do before, and kept them closed for a few moments.

Her eyes flashed open. "You fight. Long sharp cutting

thing." She held up her hand and moved it around in the air.

"This is getting nowhere," he said. "Sofia, you understand none of this makes any sense. What's more, I think you want me to take you back to my boat and put you in the water. It's the end of October here and the water is cold. I don't think this is a good idea."

Of course, nothing made any sense about Sofia, but this did not bother his attempt to problem solve. This approach had always worked for him.

Except when he lost Martha.

And didn't get the promotion.

And now he would lose Sofia, a woman who had unearthed a powerful set of emotions within him.

"I'm sick," she said.

"Stand up and turn around," Phillip said.

She stood and he approached, raising her shirt to expose her back.

"Whew," he said, stepping back. "Sofia, your skin is starting to split. Won't you let me take you to a hospital? If I put you in the water like that, I mean, you could die."

She turned around quickly.

"Please go now. I have much sickness."

He changed into heavier clothing since there was a cool northerly wind, and it would be cold on the water. Phillip gave Sofia one of his winter coats to wear and they drove out to his mooring.

His small boat was one of only three still moored in the protected cove. Phillip knew that the summer residents had already left and few of the homes along the shoreline were lived in year-round, so he was not worried about be-ing seen.

The dinghy was not a graceful craft and pulling oars was awkward with two people, but he eventually made it to his boat and tied it off to one of the cleats. Sofia climbed into his motorboat first, then he followed. He sat in one of the two captain's chairs, and she sat in the other. They looked at each other, but neither spoke.

52

"Can I wait for you?" he said.

"Wait?"

"Yes, can I wait for you to come back to the boat?"

"*Fillleeeep*, no. Too long to wait. I go far. Take a long time."

"When you come back can you get out of the water again, like you did this time?"

She looked at him sideways, concentrating.

"Not suppose to be that way," she said.

"Yes, but hang on. Let's say you go to wherever you have to go, and it takes a long time. But you come back to this spot. Can you come out of the water again, like you are now?"

"Maybe," she said.

"I might be very old," he said. "Would you be old too?"

"No, I be same."

"Oh," Phillip said.

The boat rocked gently in the wind. Two bickering gulls fought over something at the shoreline.

"Why did you have to come here?" he said. "I was doing alright before you came."

"I always come for you. Always."

"But it hurts that you're leaving now, just when I'm very happy. I don't understand how you can show up briefly, make someone happy, then leave them again."

"I come back," she said, standing up and coming across to him. "But a long time. You be old. So what? Who care?"

She kissed him hard, holding his face on both sides with her hands.

"I will miss *Fillleeeep*. Not so long this time."

He did not embrace her, afraid that he might hurt her festering back.

"I'm going to come back here the last week of October. Every October. Right here. Will you come back?"

"I come back. But long time *Fillleeeep*. You wait?"

"Of course."

She kissed him again, but not the rough, furtive pressing of lips. This time she gently pressed her slightly parted mouth onto his and left them as the little boat rocked gently. She finally drew away from him and before he could speak, she turned and dove off the boat into the water.

"Hey!" he yelled, jumping up. Looking over the side he saw a swirl of water.

Phillip stood there for several minutes until the swirl dissipated and blended into the rippled surface.

"Sofia," he said quietly.

Just when he was about to turn away from the water, he saw an article of clothing float up. It was her sweatshirt, one of her new black canvas shoes could be seen floating below the surface. Then his pair of jockey underwear appeared resting just below the surface.

He used the boat hook to grab the articles of clothing.

But that was all. She never came up. He scanned the cove and saw nothing.

53

Phillip was not the same after Sofia left.

He found another position at a branch of a large national bank two towns over. Within a year he was made manager of the branch. He realized that the work at both banks was essentially the same, though the salary was higher at the new bank.

He continued to hang out with his group of friends. His former wife Martha gave birth to twins and he was happy for the couple.

Each year he rowed out to his mooring during the last week of October. He took a book or magazine with him and sat on the boat. If there was a storm, he went out as soon as it abated.

After much pressure from Felicia, Phillip reluctantly agreed to start dating again. He met many nice women and enjoyed their company. He became very friendly with a divorcee named Susan McPherson. While Susan eagerly sought a romantic relationship with Phillip, she soon intuited that he had his mind elsewhere. Instead, they struck up a powerful Platonic friendship.

The years fell gently away like leaves off a river birch tree; several turned and fell quickly, but then in a cascade, the rest fell with alacrity.

In his early fifties, Felicia began to worry about Phillip. While he was the same old orderly, controlled, gentle, and polite Phillip, he was also prone to periods of long silence and brooding. She wondered about his mental health and in concert with her husband Ernie and Phillip's friend Susan, they staged an intervention.

He listened politely and with great respect to their entreaty that he seek counseling. They were concerned that he was suffering from depression.

Phillip agreed to see a psychotherapist, though he disagreed that he was depressed.

He did not like the first therapist he met with, but very much liked the second one, a seventy-one-year-old licensed psychologist named Dr. Stella Norman.

Dr. Norman was a remarkably small, thin woman with short, snow-white hair. She leaned dramatically forward in their 45-minute sessions and he wondered whether she was hard of hearing.

It took Phillip four sessions before he told her about Sofia. He spoke for 35 of the 45 minutes, detailing his interactions with Sofia, her proclivity for sugar, her reluctance to wear clothes, and other amusing details. He finished by explaining that he was waiting for her to return one day.

After Phillip completed his story, Dr. Norman said nothing but rocked ever so slightly in her large chair.

"Well?" Phillip said.

"Well, what?" Dr. Norman said.

"What do you think?"

"Think of what?" she said quietly.

"About Sofia."

"What about Sofia?"

"Do you think I made her up?"

"I don't know," Dr. Norman said. "Did you?"

"I don't know."

"I don't know either."

They looked at each other in silence, the only sound was from Dr. Norman's gentle unconscious rocking.

"I'm waiting for her to return."

"Yes, so I gather."

"Do you think she'll return?"

"I don't know. What do you think?"

"I think she'll return. I just don't know when. She didn't exactly give me a hard date."

"So I gather," Dr. Norman said.

"Do you think I'm crazy?" Phillip said, nervously crossing his fingers together across his knee.

"Do I think you're crazy?" Dr. Norman said. "No, I don't think you're crazy. Do you think you're crazy?"

"I think my sister thinks I'm crazy."

"She's concerned about you. That's not unusual when family members are concerned about their loved ones."

"I suppose."

"Our time is almost up today, Phillip."

"Yes. I think I talked too much."

"There's no such thing as talking too much in here," she said.

"Tell me, is it OK to be expecting Sofia to return?"

"Why not?"

"My sister says I'm wasting my life."

"Does your sister know the entire story of Sofia, or does she still think Sofia went home because she was sick. Does she know the other part about the boat?"

"No. She thinks Sofia went home. I never told her about the boat. Should I tell her that part?"

"Perhaps not."

"That's what I was thinking."

54

When Phillip turned 62, he was promoted to a senior position in the bank's regional headquarters that was a long drive from his home. It took him ninety minutes each way, and he dutifully approached the new job with a reliance on order and process.

Three years later Felicia sold her gift store and bought a retirement home in Naples, Florida. She begged Phillip to retire and join Ernie and her, but he enjoyed his work and refused to leave the area.

"You still think she's coming back, Phil, but she's not," Felicia said. "It's time to move on. Please."

But Phillip was adamant about staying on in his small town. He enjoyed going to films with Susan, playing bridge with a large group of men, and puttering around the yard.

He had also bought a slightly larger, more stable boat and spent time on it more often in the fall.

When Phillip retired at age 67 from the bank, he remained in the same house and continued his life of bridge, dinners, and movies with Susan—who now used a cane—and puttering around the yard. Two years later Ernie passed away in Florida from a sudden heart attack and Felicia moved back to the small seaside town.

"I feel more at home, here," she told Phillip. "Florida is very sunny, but everyone seems old, like me. And you."

One beautiful autumn day, Phillip dutifully rowed out to his boat in the cove. The weather was unseasonably warm, and he perspired as he rowed out to the mooring. He tied off the dinghy and wiped his forehead with the back of his hand.

He had brought a sandwich and a Diet Coke in a small backpack. He pulled a canvas folding chair from the boat's hold and sat in the sun in the aft portion. While he wanted to read, and had brought a new paperback with him, the gentle rocking and the bright sun began to wear him down.

It did not take him long to fall asleep. He was soon under a deep blanket of fleeting emotions and mild confusion.

And then he heard splashing.

Followed by a strong, distinct voice.

He tried to speak but could not get his mouth to function.

The voice was strong.

He opened his eyes.

55

"Sir. Sir, can you hear me?"

Phillip was blinded staring into the sun.

"What?" he said.

"Sir, can you hear me?"

Phillip raised his hand to shield his eyes.

"Who are you?"

"I'm Coast Guard Seaman Franklin, Sir. Are you alright?"

"Yes. Why are you asking?"

"A family member called us today and said you were not well and might be in distress on your boat. She said you were not answering your phone after many calls. She's worried about you."

"Felicia called you?"

"Yes, your sister called us. Were you sleeping, Sir?"

"Yes. I'm fine."

"Sir, can you please stand for a minute and wave to your sister? She's on the shore there next to her car."

Phillip stood, strained to see in the bright sun, and saw Felicia waving from the shore sixty yards away.

"Would you like us to take you back to shore, Sir?"

"No. I'm fine. I was just napping."

"Sorry to bother you. If you're going to stay out here alone, it would be best if you wore a life preserver. Do you have a life preserver on board?"

"Yes, but I'll get it later if you don't mind."

Phillip sat back down and watched the orange Coast Guard boat push off. He stood again quickly and waived to Felicia.

Then he sat and ate his sandwich and sipped his Diet Coke.

He read for a while, sipped his drink, and reveled in the bright October sunlight as it warmed his face.

And he fell asleep again as the sun, lower now because of its autumnal arc, moved swiftly to the west. By the time the sun fell behind the tree line, the temperature had dropped.

He woke, shivering.

Oh god, did I fall asleep again? I keep doing that.

He packed away his belongings, put away the chair, stood next to the steering wheel for a moment to gather his strength. He felt out of breath more often these days.

The cool breeze had abated, but it was still chilly. He went to the side of the boat where the dinghy was attached and gently pulled it in since it had drifted.

Phillip was surprised at how weak he felt, and he sat on

the gunwale of the boat to rest.

He looked idly around the cove, its water turning dark in the shade of the trees.

Get going before you fall asleep again.

He sighed, gathered his strength, and lowered the backpack into the dinghy. It was increasingly tricky to get in and out of the dinghy, given his achy joints and unreliable sense of balance.

Phillip grunted as he tried to raise his right leg over the gunwale and into the unsteady dinghy. He stopped, straddled across the gunwale, one leg dangling above the dinghy, the other on the solid deck of the boat.

He sat that way for a moment but felt weak and uncertain. He fell onto the deck of the boat, landing on his back with a stunning thud. He lay there disoriented for a moment. It was a strangely peaceful place to be, he realized. Staring up at the clear, ice-blue sky he was content, though still a little cold.

Phillip smiled, though he was not sure why.

Maybe I'll just rest here for a while.

56

"Are you sick?"

He heard the voice and turned his head toward the raised outboard motor.

Her hair was wet and plastered against her forehead. Her elbows were over the rear transom holding her up out of the water.

Phillip lay on his back in the boat, his head turned to look at her.

"Are you sick?" she repeated.

"I don't know," he said, turning back to look at the sky above.

"You look sick," she said.

"Maybe I am."

"I came back," she said.

"I know."

"You are old," she said. "I can see you are sick."

"I'm OK," he said. "But I am tired."

He heard a great deal of splashing and slapping, like someone clapping wet hands.

"*Fillleeeep,*" she said, her face next to his.

He turned to look at her.

"You're old," he said.

"I make myself old like you," she said. "Do you like?"

"Yes." He leaned away from her and saw that she was indeed older, thinner but still beautiful. Her hair was dark with streaks of gray, though it was hard to tell in the dimming light. She was naked and he could feel the water that she brought in had started to soak into his sweatshirt.

"You have legs," he said.

"Yes. For you."

He turned to stare up at the sky again. They lay there in the cool, late afternoon air, the boat barely rocking.

"I am cold," she said.

"Yes. Of course." He struggled to get up, starting with one elbow, then rolled to his knees, and finally stood up.

"You are sick," she said.

"I suppose. Does it matter?"

"No."

He stumbled into the cabin and found an old, wrinkled rain jacket and an older beach towel.

"Here," he said. "You should put on the jacket and put a towel around your waist."

She stood up and put on the jacket and towel. Phillip was amazed at how she had aged, her breasts were smaller, her frame seemed to have thinned. Her cheekbones were more pronounced, but her eyes were still blazing fireballs of energy.

"You look beautiful," he said.

"You are handsome."

He laughed. "I'm old."

"But handsome."

"Where have you been all these years?" he said.

She shrugged.

"I see," he said. "You can't tell me where you go. But can I tell you where I imagined you went?"

"Tell me."

"I imagined you went to Ireland, Scotland, the Spanish coast, Normandy, and on to Italy. Then around the boot to the Mediterranean and to Greece. Or something like that."

"You're funny."

He sighed.

"It's great to see you again."

She took a step forward and put her arms around his chest, hugging him tightly.

"I kiss you now," she said, pulling away and reaching up with her hands to bookend his face.

They kissed and he tasted the salty water on her face.

"You should sit down," she said. "You are sick."

He did not disagree and sat down on the deck.

"Tell me," he said. "Are you really old like me, or did you just become that way to make me feel better?"

"You're funny."

"Well, which is it?"

"I tell you I change for you."

"That was kind of you. But you're still beautiful old or young."

They sat on the deck as the sun fell farther back toward the horizon, sending long shadows across the cove.

"What sickness do you have?" she asked, snuggled up hard against his body.

"I don't know. I think it's my heart. I always feel weak. Today I feel drained."

"What is 'drained'?"

He laughed. "It feels like all the water is leaking out of me."

"Oh," she said. "Is it a bad feeling?"

"No, not bad."

"Are you sad?"

"Not today. I'm very happy today. You are here. I waited a long time."

"We will meet many more times," she said.

"You said that before," he said, coughing a little. "I don't understand. You said we keep seeing each other, only you remember the meetings and I don't. Is that right?"

"You forget. I *never* forget."

"OK. So, why did we meet today? This time. I don't get it. This isn't like the other times, is it?"

"No. You make me come back. Never before do you say that. So, I come back this time."

"Why did you come back?"

"Why?" She thought a little about that, looking idly up at the sky that was now darker. A single star poked through in the east as sunset neared.

"I come back because this is the best you. I like you much this way. Other times you are different. Not so nice. This you is the best you."

"I suppose that's a compliment," he said.

She turned to him, held his face in her hands, and kissed him gently.

He lay back on the deck, staring at the darkening sky.

He was very tired but very happy.

Later that night the Coast Guard returned after Felicia reported Phillip's car remained parked near the mooring and his dinghy was still attached to the boat.

Phillip's body was found lying on the deck. Next to him were a beach towel and rain jacket.

There was some confusion about the circumstances of his death since there was a great deal of saltwater on the deck and the beach towel was saturated. Later, authorities determined that Phillip Preston, a 69-year-old, retired bank executive, became confused after a cardiac event while tending to his boat. He used a towel to sop up saltwater on the boat's deck and suffered a fatal heart attack.

Many strange things in life cannot be explained.

It is that way now, and it has always been that way.

MORE FROM KEITH YOCUM

A Whisper Came

THE LIGHTHOUSE HOLDS A SECRET

Stacie, a young ambitious reporter is sent to Chatham on Cape Cod to follow up on the body of an unidentified woman found floating nearby. Over the centuries Cape Cod has been the site of thousands of shipwrecks leaving the sandy shore littered with debris, legends, and ghost stories. Stacie's editors encourage her to dig into the mix of Chatham's quirky residents and to write about the mysteries surrounding the old Monomoy Point Lighthouse. On a lark, she makes a nighttime visit to the lighthouse with a young charter boat captain and in the process, stumbles tragically into a dark mystery that forces her to question her sanity and the truth buried in a legend.

Color of Blood

(BOOK 1 OF THE DENNIS CUNNINGHAM SERIES)

Dennis is glad to be back at work. His wife's death left him devastated but he'll do anything to lose himself into work at the Inspector General's office of the CIA. A brilliant, if prickly investigator, he's spent his career chasing down the Agency's thieves and liars. When his boss forces him to take a low-level assignment to investigate a missing employee in Australia, he soon finds that even in the red dust of the Outback, there is romance – and death – just a sweltering heartbeat away.

A *Dark Place*

(BOOK 2 OF THE DENNIS CUNNINGHAM SERIES)

An old case spills new blood. Dennis loves policing the CIA's network of spies for liars and thieves. But each time he plows into a case, it's harder for him to keep alive his relationship with Judy, an Aussie cop and the only woman who understands his passions and quirks. When Dennis and Judy meet in London to rekindle their relationship, they are sucked into the city's dark underworld. To save Judy's life Dennis must solve two cases simultaneously. If you like non-stop action, dark humor and complicated heroes, then you'll love A *Dark Place*.

Valley of Spies

(BOOK 3 OF THE DENNIS CUNNINGHAM SERIES)

When an American woman vanishes in New Zealand, it perplexes authorities. There is no body, no witness and no motive. But what looks like a sad, unfortunate case of foul play, slowly turns into something darker. The missing tourist is a female psychologist under contract from the CIA to see employees in strictest confidence. Was her disappearance a random act of violence, or an act of international espionage? Does someone want to know her patients' dark, dirty secrets? Dennis Cunningham, the gruff but uncanny CIA investigator, is tugged out of early retirement in Western Australia to rubber stamp a foregone conclusion by the agency about the real perpetrators. A brilliant but unusual sleuth, Cunningham can't help but pick at the agency's scab on this case until it bleeds red all over.

Daniel

STRANGE THINGS HAPPEN IN WAR – BUT VIETNAM WAS ALWAYS DIFFERENT

In January 1972, during the waning days of that sad war, a lone soldier crawled through the barbed wire and entered an isolated American firebase. He said his name was Daniel Carson, but a quick check found that a soldier with the same name and physical description was already buried at Arlington National Cemetery. Who was this new soldier named Daniel? Was he a crazy man, a common deserter or something else entirely? And why did he have such a profound effect on the unlucky company of grunts trying to survive the last days of the war? As a fierce regiment of North Vietnamese regulars prepares to destroy the forgotten hilltop firebase, the odd little soldier named Daniel seems to have all the answers to their survival. Several years after the war, three survivors of the firebase meet in Washington, D.C. and, almost by accident, discover the shocking truth about Daniel.

Titus

DURING CARNAGE IN THE CIVIL WAR,
IS THERE A SERIAL MURDERER AT WORK?

A Union soldier is found dead on the outskirts of camp, his neck sliced open from ear to ear. But when more soldiers are found with their throats slit, an uneasy mood falls over the Union regiment. Who is killing these soldiers, and what does the strange mark on the dead men's foreheads mean? A young Union lieutenant and an eccentric field surgeon are ordered to get to the bottom of the killings. Can the two officers unmask the killer and motive before the fog of battle hides his identity forever?

Miraflores — Memoir of a Young Spy

A NEWLY MINTED SPY FIGHTS HIS ADVERSARIES—
BOTH INTERNAL AND EXTERNAL—
IN THIS COLD WAR THRILLER

At the height of the Cold War, young Nick Halliday joins the CIA to distance himself from a family tragedy and to do his part in the patriotic fight against the communist menace. Rushed into his first undercover assignment in Panama in 1958, Nick finds himself mired in the humid, dripping world of deceit and lies. Pretending to be a leftist-leaning visiting professor at the University of Panama, Nick infiltrates an earnest, naïve group of leftist students bent on Panama regaining ownership of the canal. But

Nick's budding romance with Maria, a beautiful student activist, throws his mission sideways. The international clash of ideologies harshly intrudes on a young man's love for a woman. Both are expendable pawns in a vast world-wide deathmatch. Can they survive in a game that only values winning, whatever the cost? And what does winning mean, anyway?

KEITH YOCUM lives on Cape Cod. He has worked for *The Boston Globe* and *The New England Journal of Medicine*. He is the author of eight novels and welcomes feedback at www.keithyocum.com.